ONE LAST DANCE WITH LAWRENCE WELK
AND
OTHER STORIES

ONE LAST DANCE WITH LAWRENCE WELK
AND
OTHER STORIES

by

Peter Damian Bellis

River Boat Books   **St. Paul, MN 55165**

One Last Dance With Lawrence Welk and Other Stories is an original publication of River Boat Books. The stories in this collection have never before appeared in book form. These stories are works of fiction. Any similarities to actual persons or events is purely coincidental.

River Boat Books
P.O. Box 65314
St. Paul, MN 55165-0314

Copyright © 1997 by Peter Damian Bellis
Published by arrangement with the author.
Library of Congress Catalog Card Number: 96-70860
ISBN: 0-9654756-0-3 (Trade paperback)

First River Boat Books Printing, November, 1996

For Little Grandmother

And Nana

Acknowledgments

 First and foremost I would like to thank my wife, Kathleen, and my children, Rachael and Andrew, for their patience and support, and I would like to thank my mom for the computer and my dad for sharing with me his understanding of literature, gleaned from over thirty years of teaching college English courses, and also for his keen critical eye. I would also like to thank my agent, Kip Kotzen, and my publisher, Jim McVeety, for their encouragement and faith.

Contents

One Last Dance With Lawrence Welk

My dad always said Mrs. Rottweiler was as crazy as a loon, but she didn't mean any harm, which was his way of saying you had to help her out whenever you could. He said it was a Catholic's duty to help out those less fortunate, and that went double for crazies, loonies, pick any word you want. So there he was, my dad, the patron saint of fruitcakes, checking in on Mrs. Rottweiler once every couple of weeks, and then he started dragging me with cause he thought I needed a few lessons in being neighborly. Well, maybe I did. But I sure didn't want a whole lot to do with an old women who smelled of Fisherman's lozenges and Vick's Vapor Rub and wore a Holy Rosary around her neck so you could see it. What if the Klein boys saw me at Mrs. Rottweiler's? You can bet the word would get around then. I tried to point this out to my dad, maybe we could pick some other neighbor, but he didn't see it. "What are you thinking, Buddy boy? The truth is you don't go picking your neighbors. No, the truth is you don't have any say in the matter, so you might as well get used to them. Who knows," and then he laughed, " you might even grow to like them." My dad was born in the house we lived in. My dad, the great believer in neighbors.

Going to Mrs. Rottweiler's eventually became a kind of routine, like delivering the mail. Every other Saturday morning my dad would box up a few tools, and I'd be standing right behind him watching him do it, and then we'd head out the door, me in my Dodger's baseball cap, cause my mom was from Brooklyn, a couple of bluebirds up in a tree somewhere, you could hear them twirping at us as we went by, the two of us trudging through the backyard and past the row of dying Lombardy poplars my mom had planted to mark the property line, down the dirt alley and past the Gruber's and that patch of corn they called their Winter Bonanza, and then there was Mrs. Rottweiler's, the back of it, a small, two bedroom bungalow and an unattached garage, both with aluminum siding from the sixties, both a bright, lime green color that seemed to glow even in the middle of the sunniest day. Whenever I went over to Mrs. Rottweiler's I thought of radiation sickness and mobile homes. Of course my dad wasn't of the same opinion. He told me Mrs. Rottweiler's house was built more than half a century ago, or thereabouts, a house they got mail-order special from Sears, like you could get a bicycle today. They sure didn't build houses like that anymore. My dad was also a great believer in Sears.

Mrs. Rottweiler was a big-boned German-type woman, square hips, a square jaw, and big, jowly arms. Every day she wore the same thing, or at least every time I saw her. A threadbare, pale blue housecoat dotted all over with something like peacocks, a pair of white tennies, and a pair of nylon stockings which never made it up from her ankles.

Her husband had been dead for something like thirty years. Died somewhere in the Pacific during World War II. On an island, I guess. I don't think Mrs. Rottweiler remembered he was dead, or sometimes, if he had ever been alive. In fact, most of the time Mrs. Rottweiler didn't seem to remember much of anything. She certainly had trouble remembering who we were. Every time we showed up on the back steps and my dad knocking on the screen door, she just stood there looking out through the window, carefully holding the chintzy, flower-patterned curtain up so only her eyes could be seen through the glass. Then she'd ask us what we wanted and my dad would start to explain how we lived down a couple of houses on the other side of the alley, we were neighbors, just come by to see how she was doing, didn't she recognize my dad, he used to play with her boy, Winston.

"No, no for sure, Winston's not here. Winston's down in Rochester."

"Course he is, Mrs. Rottweiler. But I didn't come about Winston."

"You didn't, eh. What is it you said you wanted? You're not trying to sell me any encyclopedias, are you. Is that what you're doing? Ach! If you're doing that you better go home. I'm not buying."

"No, Mrs. Rottweiler. We're not trying to sell you anything. We're the Sundquists. I'm Hank Sundquist, Mrs. Rottweiler. And this is my boy, Buddy."

"He's too small. How old did you say he was?"

"He's ten years old, Mrs. Rottweiler."

"Well he never played with my son Winston. My son Winston turned thirty-seven last March. Ach, you think I don't know how old my own son is?"

"No, Mrs. Rottweiler. I didn't mean Buddy played with your son. No, I meant myself. I played with Winston. Me. Henry Sundquist."

"Ach. Is that what you meant. I see."

That's how it would go, sometimes for as long as twenty minutes. Then Mrs. Rottweiler would break off talking, her lips sputtering a bit but no sound coming out and her eyes blinking like she'd been watching t.v. in the dark and all of a sudden the lights came on. Then she'd jerk the curtain back and the door would open and she'd be smiling this square-jawed smile you'd swear was nailed to her face. Of course she remembered Henry Sundquist, and was this his little boy, Buddy, her tweaking my ears now and the smell of Vick's Vapor Rub and the lozenges clogging my throat. My how the years go by.

The very next thing my dad would be puttering about the place, see what needed doing, and I'd be puttering right along behind him. One day maybe her lawn mower needed fixing. She was always breaking her lawn mower. She'd mow over anything, rocks as big as potatoes, bottles some of the Klein boys had tossed into her yard on their way to school, even a dead cat if she didn't see it. The next time maybe her gutters were stuffed full of moldy leaves and wet twigs from the half dozen elm trees huddling over her house, which meant when it rained the water came straight down the lime green aluminum siding and worked its way into the basement. My dad would set me up on the ladder and give me a garden trowel for the gutters, and a handkerchief to wipe my face, and then he'd pop down into the basement with a mop and a bucket. After we were done Mrs. Rottweiler would sit us down at the kitchen table and serve up some tuna salad sandwiches, and we'd eat them in spite of they smelled like the lozenges and the Vick's on top of the fish and mayonnaise, which is a lot worse than any regular fish smell, I can tell you that. Like stabbing you in the stomach.

Seems like something always struck you peculiar when you were over at Mrs. Rottweiler's. Just ask anybody. But I got to tell you there was one time had to beat all the rest put together. It was late November, and cold, and the sky already had that winter's here look with the clouds all ruffled like feathers and mostly gray with patches of white, looked like a flock of pigeons coming down to roost. Me and my dad hadn't even made it past Mrs. Rottweiler's garage when she burst out through the door, her pale blue housecoat unbuttoned and the peacocks flapping about and her old ladies underwear staring me in the face. She almost fell down the steps, except her right arm sort of got itself wrapped around the railing, and then she gave a jerk and righted herself and sat down on the bottom step, rigid, inarticulate, her exposed knees turning pink from cold and exertion and her face pink and her breath coming out in short, frosty gasps. How come she didn't fall and break both her legs I'll never know. You're always hearing about old folks tripping over a crack in their driveway and falling down and then both their legs are broke and they never walk again. But Mrs. Rottweiler didn't break anything, not even a toe. Of course you couldn't tell that at first. My dad leaned over to help her up, but she wouldn't budge. It was like all her weight had sunk itself into that step. Like she was made of cement herself. But nothing was broke. Then she said something I didn't quite hear, and my dad ran into the house.

The next thing I knew I heard my dad banging around in Mrs. Rottweiler's bedroom, at least he was on that side of the house, and then he was yelling, and then cursing, and then I heard a smash like a glass lamp being knocked to the floor, but I figured my dad would holler if he needed some help, so I didn't budge neither. But I did start wondering about that smashed-lamp sound. I thought maybe it was this red-glass table lamp Mrs. Rottweiler had, with two green-eyed tigers painted on the bottom and a gold colored shade. It looked kind of Oriental. I remember my dad telling me how Mr. Rottweiler had probably sent it from the Pacific. Before he was killed. My dad said it might have been the last thing she ever got from Mr. Rottweiler. "That's what it's all about, Buddy boy," he said. "Sends her a lamp from halfway around the world. That's what love'll do for you." My dad, the great believer in sending lamps. Funny thing was, Mrs. Rottweiler didn't seem all that bothered by her lamp maybe getting broke. Like I said before, I don't think she really remembered her dead husband. She just sat there, unmoved, silent, her lips turning purple in the cold, almost like she was dead herself.

That's when I went inside. It wasn't that I was spooked or anything, I just didn't want her to flop down dead right there in front of me, and I had the strangest feeling that if I kept looking at her sitting there like she was with that look of a tombstone, she was going to do just that. So I went inside and sat down at the kitchen table to wait for my dad to finish up or call for help. I don't remember how long I sat there, but I do remember the kitchen smelled more of Fisherman's lozenges and Vick's than Mrs. Rottweiler herself, and I started thinking how that old lady smell of hers got into everything. The longer you were around it, the deeper it went. I tried to smell my own skin, but I couldn't tell, but I figured it was there all the same. I was probably carrying that smell in my bloodstream. I thought I was going to have people calling me an old lady the next thing I knew. The Klein boys for certain. They could smell out a dead cat before it was even dead yet. Just ask anybody. Then I saw the cake, a chocolate bakery cake set out for show on the counter and the box tossed in the garbage. I wondered who brought Mrs. Rottweiler a cake. I wondered if the cake smelled of lozenges and Vick's. I wondered if the smell mattered all that much when you were eating it.

I was still thinking about that cake when I heard my dad bang his way out of Mrs. Rottweiler's bedroom, down the hall, and then he went stumbling into the living room-slash-dining-room, a dirty, yellowish sofa on one side with white doilies stuck on the arms and the fuzz beading up and a roll-away t.v. pulled out from the wall, and on the other side, smack up against the back of that sofa, a heavily polished maplewood table, with a Planter's Peanut jar in the middle crammed full of dead pussy willows. I could see my dad from the kitchen. He was standing with his back to me on the other side of the sofa, and breathing so heavy it sounded like whistling. He had a ratty old Jack Kramer tennis racquet in his hand, and he was looking up at the ceiling, something was up there, but I couldn't see what because of the wall. Then it was like he felt me looking at him and his back stiffened some and he caught his breath, and for a moment I thought I should have waited outside with Mrs. Rottweiler. Maybe he wanted some more time alone with whatever it was so he could finish. My dad always said you should finish what you started. But then he turned part ways around and saw me sitting there in the kitchen and he nodded for me to join him.

"It's an owl, Buddy boy," he said. He was still kind of whistling when he talked, and his whole face all the way back to his ears had a sleek, sweaty, kind of oily shine about it from banging around in Mrs. Rottweiler's bedroom. "I've been having an awful time. No wonder Mrs. Rottweiler came running out like she did. You wouldn't think an owl would put up such a fight, would you? But this one sure is a fighter. Good thing you came inside, Buddy boy. I'm going to need your help."

"What should I do?" I said.

"Go open the front door. And keep it open. I'll chase him out with this racquet. But watch yourself when he's flying around, Buddy boy. He already came at me once. In the hall. There's no predicting what he might do. If it comes to that we might have to kill him."

The owl was sitting up on top of a white pine bookcase in the corner of the room. It was staring down at my dad and the racquet, but it didn't move, it just sat there, panting, its wings ruffled out like it was drying off, and every now and then it would give a little squeak. I headed for the door, but I wasn't moving too fast on account of my eyes were fixed to that owl. I mean you don't want to take a chance have one swooping down on top of you. Talons raking across your face. You could maybe lose an eye that way. That's what my dad meant when he told me to watch myself. According to him there were hundreds of ways you could lose your eye, and the only way you could keep both of them was by watching yourself. He was always talking about it. I think maybe he had a brother once who lost an eye. I don't remember how. All I know is my dad believed in watching yourself.

"Get ready," he said.

The next thing I knew I was outside, behind the open screen door, one hand holding onto the handle and the other braced against the lime green aluminum siding. It seemed colder than before, and I wondered if Mrs. Rottweiler was all right or if she had flopped down dead anyway. Her whole face was probably purple by now. Then I wondered what was taking my dad so long. I couldn't see him. From where I was, all I could see was the back of the sofa and the heavily polished maplewood table and the Planter's Peanut jar with the pussy willows. Then I heard a whoop or something, maybe it was a cough, and then I could hear my dad banging that ratty Jack Kramer against the bookcase and shouting, and the owl was squeaking all the while, but it didn't fly out. Then the owl flew into the dining room part and landed on the table. You don't realize how small an owl is until you see one up close. This one looked about half the size of a mushball. It went and ducked behind the Planter's jar and then stopped, but you could see its eyes blinking through the branches of the dead pussy willows. You could tell no one had chased it around with a tennis racquet before.

Then my dad sailed past. I say sailed because that's what he did. I don't know what he was trying to do. He must have tripped or something. But there he went sailing through the air, right over the back of the sofa, and then he landed square on his back on top of that maplewood table and sailed all the way across. It was sort of funny to watch it. Like watching a slow motion instant replay on the *Wide World of Sports*. My dad sailing across that table and the Planter's Peanut jar getting knocked off and the dead pussy willow branches going everywhere, and that little owl flying straight up from the commotion, but then sort of just hanging there in the air, like it was hanging from the end of a wire, and then my dad was right underneath. You could tell by the way he was looking up at that owl what he had in mind. He swung that ratty Jack Kramer as hard as he could and there was a little pop like when a tennis ball splits, and then that little owl sailed straight into the kitchen, and my dad sailed off the end of that maplewood table and smacked right into Mrs. Rottweiler's antique china cupboard.

"Boy, you sure got him, dad!"

I came inside. I picked up the Planter's Peanut jar and put it on the table. There were dead pussy willow branches all over the floor, but I stepped on them anyway. My dad was sitting up against the china cupboard, looking at that ratty Jack Kramer, and rubbing his jaw. The strings were busted, and my dad had a funny look on his face. It was almost a smile, but there was something sour about it, too. Like he was happy enough he had knocked that little owl into the kitchen, but he had busted the strings of the Jack Kramer to do it.

"Do you think you killed him?"

"I think I might have, Buddy boy. I think I did."

You wouldn't believe what happened to that owl. There he was smack dab dead in the middle of that chocolate cake. There wasn't any blood, which I guess maybe that bird had broken his neck. Me and my dad didn't know what to say. We just stood there and stared a while at that owl mashed into the cake. He was mashed in there pretty deep, beak first, and the rest of the cake spread out around him. I remember thinking the cake and that owl together and the way the feathers were sticking straight up and splattered with little bits of chocolate icing, it looked like one of those Sunday hats you see old ladies wear in church. The kind of hat maybe Mrs. Rottweiler would wear. Then I remember wondering again what had happened to Mrs. Rottweiler. And then there she was, standing behind us like my thinking her name had brought her in. She had buttoned up her peacocks. And her knees were still pink, but that was about it. She was German. She wasn't bothered by the cold.

"See here, Henryzundquist." When Mrs. Rottweiler remembered who my dad was she called him Henryzundquist, just like that with a "z," and like it was one word, too. "I asked you to get that bird out of my house. Not to kill it."

"Yes, Mrs. Rottweiler. I know you did. Sure. But there wasn't any other way."

Mrs. Rottweiler thought about that. Then she gave a lozengey smelling "hrumpf" and said she hadn't asked for a dead owl, ach, you could bet your life the cats would dig it out of the garbage can, just as soon as the sun went down they would, ach, the best thing would be to bury it in the back yard, eh, what do you think Henryzundquist, eh, put a small stone over the grave to keep the cats out, sure thing, sure, and maybe say a prayer or two, Godt wouldn't mind, Godt liked prayers, you betcha he did, and who could say, maybe that little owl had a soul just like the rest of us here, sure he did, ach, there wasn't born a man or woman who could say he didn't.

I had never in my whole life heard Mrs. Rottweiler say so much at one time. And crazy talk, too. Loony as a loon talk. Pick whatever word you want. My dad must have been thinking the same thing because he was just staring at her with his head cocked to one side like some droopy old basset hound about to flop down dead. You didn't surprise

my dad all that often, but when you did, you could tell.
Then Mrs. Rottweiler smiled at the both us, the owl, too, for
all I knew. She just stood there smiling and the peacocks
on her housecoat seemed to be smiling too. And then she
glided over to the garbage and fished out the empty cake
box, and I say glided because it looked like she was being
pulled along by strings. Like angels in those Christmas
plays. I'm not even sure her feet touched the floor. Then
she was back at the counter and she plucked out the owl
and brushed away the crumbs and then put it in the box,
smoothing out its feathers as she did so. She closed the lid
carefully and fixed it with tape and then gave it to me, and
without a word she glided back to the garbage can and
dumped what was left of the chocolate cake. Of course I
wanted to say something when she did that. I mean she
could have cut out the bad spot and saved the rest. I'd have
eaten it. If I'd have eaten a cake that smelled like
Fisherman's lozenges and Vick's Vapor Rub, you could
have bet money I'd have eaten a cake that had an owl
mashed into it. But I didn't say a word. Holding that dead
owl boxed up like it was kind of took the words right out of
me.

Then we went outside. My dad dug a small hole at the
base of a stone bird bath in the middle of the back yard, but
it took him a while. It was colder than before and the
ground was hard and he had to chip away at it like ice.
Mrs. Rottweiler had picked the spot because she liked
birds, but no birds ever came to wash in her bird bath. The
summer before my dad had fixed a couple of plastic

bluebirds along the rim so she could pretend, and that was it for birds until the owl. I put the box in the hole and then my dad covered it up with the chips of dirt and a cinder block on top, to keep out the cats, and then Mrs. Rottweiler said we should say a prayer. We said the *Our Father*, and when we got to the part about forgiving those who trespassed against us, Mrs. Rottweiler gave my dad a sharp look, like everything he'd done that morning had been a sin, the smashed lamp, busting the strings of that Jack Kramer, and the owl, of course, all the way from killing it to my dad acting surprised when she said we should bury it.

It was at that point, I guess you could say, that Mrs. Rottweiler forgot it was a dead owl underneath that bird bath. We finished saying our prayer and were thinking that was it, but Mrs. Rottweiler didn't think so. She started dabbing at her eyes with a green Kleenex and said the one thing she'd always liked at funerals was music. Why wasn't there any music? Then she put the Kleenex away and told us to wait, she'd be back in a jiff, and then she disappeared up the back steps into her house. Five minutes later a window near the back opened and we could hear polka music, softly at first, but then louder. Mrs. Rottweiler had put on a scratchy old Lawrence Welk record. Me and my dad looked at each other. He looked like an usher the way he was holding that shovel against his side. I probably looked like an usher, too. Then Mrs. Rottweiler came dancing back out the back door. But she didn't look at us. I don't even know if she remembered we were there. She danced a couple of times around the bird bath and me and my dad standing there like ushers, and then she danced back to the open window, I guess so she could hear better, and then there she was, taking her short little polka steps, and keeping close to the window. Me and my dad watched her for a while. Then my dad set the shovel against the bird bath and took me home. That was the first time I ever saw Mrs. Rottweiler dancing.

The summer after the dead owl and the discarded chocolate cake, me and some of the other boys from our side of town started a baseball team. We didn't have a name. We had just finished the fifth grade. Jimmy Lundgren played first, partly because he had to be standing almost stock-still to catch a ball, but mostly because he was the biggest. He was almost six feet tall, without shoes on, and he probably weighed more than any three of us put together. In school, whenever we did a play, Jimmy Lundgren was usually a tree or some other immovable, unspeaking object, because of the way he loomed over the rest of us. Every year Mrs. Phillips said Jimmy's size would distract the audience from the other actors, and from the story itself, and so she had no choice but to cast him as a piece of scenery. But it was different with baseball. We made Jimmy our captain, and we let him play where he wanted, which was square on top of the first base bag. We settled for the leftovers. I ended up at short. Carl Reber and Todd Schneider alternated between second and third. Tommy Schultz pitched and his cousin Alfred caught. And the Klein boys played in the outfield.

Now the reason I'm bringing this up about our baseball team is that we played most of our games in the vacant lot next to Mrs. Rottweiler's. I don't think she was exactly a fan. The day after we started playing there, she had a chain link fence put up the length of her yard. She also had it spray-painted a bright, lime green, to match her house. Then she came out to watch, but, like I said, she wasn't exactly a fan. She'd come out there with a glove and stand herself smack up against that fence, and whenever anybody hit a foul her way she'd catch it and then dash into her house, her peacocks flapping, and then before anybody else got a crack at a bat she'd be back at the fence. My dad said she didn't want anybody hitting a baseball into her geraniums. He agreed with her, too. What I say is Mrs. Rottweiler had a God-awful lot of geraniums. Five truck tires stuffed full. And I don't know that a baseball or two would have done that much to mess them up either, but we never found out. In the first four weeks of that summer, Mrs. Rottweiler collected eleven balls, and the only thing my dad did about it was to suggest we hit the other way. My dad, it turns out, was also a great believer in other people's geraniums.

At first I didn't want to admit to my teammates that I knew Mrs. Rottweiler. I kept my mouth shut. Of course the first couple of balls she caught nobody said a word. We were all pretty much struck by her skill with a glove. But by the third ball Carl Reber was cursing under his breath and then biting his lip, and by the fourth ball the Klein boys said they were going to toss a few dead cats into Mrs.

Rottweiler's geraniums and see what she thought about that. By the fifth ball we began plotting how to get our baseballs back, and that's when I mentioned about my dad checking in on Mrs. Rottweiler, and me going with. I didn't say exactly that I knew her, but I gave in that I knew a little something about how peculiar she was. She had probably chucked those baseballs in a pillow case and tied the end in a knot and stuffed the whole thing in the meat freezer in her basement like it was a turkey for Thanksgiving, I said. That's when the team voted Jimmy Lundgren out of being captain and me in. Even Jimmy said it was a good idea. As captain I was supposed to find out where exactly Mrs. Rottweiler had put those baseballs and then get them back. My teammates said they'd give me whatever help I needed. They said they hoped I didn't get caught.

It took me to the end of July to find those baseballs. The first Saturday I looked in the basement, but there wasn't anything but a few packs of pork sausage and a couple of buckets of Kemps ice cream in the meat freezer. There weren't any baseballs anywhere. I even climbed into the old coal bin in back of the furnace. The next Saturday I tried her closets, but in one it was mostly just sheets and blankets, and some towels with peacocks just like her housecoat, and in another there were a couple of old cookie tins filled with nails and screws, and there was part of an old vacuum cleaner and a shoe box with some shoe polish, and in her bedroom closet there was a bunch of old lumberjack sweaters, that's what my mom would have called them, and they smelled of lozenges and Vick's in spite of their being loaded down with moth balls, and also there was that red-glass lamp with the tigers on it, except all you could see was part of one tiger, the top half of his head and one eye, because the rest of it was smashed, and packed away on the top shelf was an old army duffel bag, which I guess had probably been Mr. Rottweiler's before he died in the Pacific. But there weren't any baseballs anywhere I looked.

Then it was the last Saturday in July, which was the day I found those baseballs. Or maybe I should say they found me, cause I had already stopped looking. What happened was I was sitting on the back steps watching my dad. He was trying to put a lightning rod on Mrs. Rottweiler's garage because she was afraid it might get hit and catch fire and then everything, the garage, her house, the stone birdbath with the two plastic bluebirds on it and the dead owl underneath, all of it would go up. My dad was having one God-awful time of it wrestling with that lightning rod, and I was just sitting there watching him and wondering just how long it would take for aluminum siding to burn when I heard the sound of Lawrence Welk coming out of Mrs. Rottweiler's house. It was the same record she had put on with the owl. The next thing that happened I was standing in the doorway of the kitchen looking out past the dining room table and the dirty yellowish sofa, and there was Mrs. Rottweiler dancing her little polka steps and twirling around, and the peacocks on her housecoat were twirling around, too, and there wasn't all that much room there, even if the roll-away t.v. was pushed up against the wall, but Mrs. Rottweiler didn't seem to mind. Then the music became louder. I didn't see where it was coming from or if Mrs. Rottweiler had turned it up. It was just all of a sudden louder. And then Mrs. Rottweiler, it was like she couldn't help herself with the music so loud. She started twirling around past the corner of the sofa by the front door and then down alongside the heavily polished maplewood table. You could see the blur of her dancing reflected in the wood, like it was some kind of grainy old home-movie from when she was younger. It was almost like she was a young girl. Then she was sweeping around the end of the table and making her way back towards the sofa and she went right past me humming to the music and her eyes half-closed and her peacocks twirling faster than ever. I don't think she even knew I was standing there.

That's when I saw the baseballs. They were smack dab in the middle of that maplewood table. The Planter's Peanut jar was gone and so were the dead pussy willows, and instead there was a wicker basket or a wicker bowl or something and the baseballs were clumped together inside it, like Mrs. Rottweiler had forgotten they were baseballs altogether and thought maybe they were apples. I stared at the table a while and wondered how I hadn't seen the baseballs before. I wondered if maybe they hadn't been there all summer and that loony old Mrs. Rottweiler laughing herself silly all the while I was looking through her meat freezer or her closets. Then I looked at Mrs. Rottweiler again, and she was back dancing in between the sofa and the roll-away t.v. and doing her little polka steps now cause the music was back down. I was sure she didn't see me. I would have bet the baseballs. Then Mrs. Rottweiler turned slightly and was dancing for a moment with her back to the heavily polished maplewood table. I grabbed the wicker basket and fled.

For the rest of the summer we played our baseball without the threat of Mrs. Rottweiler. We learned to hit away from the fence and maybe messing up her geraniums. And she stopped coming out to watch. But all the same I kind of wished she would show up just once so we could keep her standing there with an empty glove. But she didn't show, and then me and my dad we stopped going over to her house and I thought it was all because of me stealing back those baseballs. I thought maybe Mrs. Rottweiler had seen me do it and was angry and had told my dad to keep me home, she didn't want to keep company with a known thief, she wanted nothing more to do with me. That's what I thought she had told my dad, but he didn't say anything about it if she did. By the end of August I didn't know what to think.

Then it was the Sunday just before Labor Day. It was early evening and the sun was just beginning to set so the sky was still a pale blue, like the color of Mrs. Rottweiler's housecoat. My dad came up to my room and rapped a quick, hard rap on my door, which meant he had something serious to say. He was silent for a moment, to let the hard rap sink in, and then he cleared the loose gravel from his throat and said, "Buddy boy, it's about Mrs. Rottweiler. I want to talk to you about Mrs. Rottweiler." Then all of a sudden he was standing in the doorway and I was sitting on the edge of my bed and the orangey, setting-sun sunlight was pouring in through the window and cutting across my dad's face, and you couldn't really see his face because of the light, it was mostly shadow, like a grainy old face in an old photograph and you can't make out who it is, and then he was speaking, the words kind of stumbling out of him into the light, and he told me how Mrs. Rottweiler was dead, she'd been in the hospital the past month and she'd died the day before, and then he said he was proud of me the way I'd learned to be neighborly, that took some growing up on my part, he was glad to see it, and then he said how her son Winston was going to be at the house the next day trying to clear through some of her things and how we were going to stop by and express our sympathy.

I have to say now that I didn't really hear what my dad was saying. The words came to me later, but they didn't register then. All the while my dad was talking, all I saw was a sort of parade of everything that had happened with me and Mrs. Rottweiler, and my dad was in it too, but it was all mixed up, twisted, bent, like something out of *The Twilight Zone*. First there was the owl and that ratty, Jack Kramer, and the owl was dead, but it was still squeaking, and old Jack was talking from his picture on the racquet, but you couldn't hear a word he was saying, and then it was Mrs. Rottweiler standing on the back steps and her peacocks were flapping and her knees were turning pink from the cold and then her face, and then she was holding up a chocolate cake and the cake smelled like lozenges and Vick's so she threw it in the garbage, and I went to fish it out but all there was was a bunch of dead cats the Klein boys had left, and then it was me and my dad and Mrs. Rottweiler in her back yard and we were dancing around that stone bird bath to the music of Lawrence Welk, and me and my dad were wearing housecoats the same as Mrs. Rottweiler and trying to do a polka, and then there she was, Mrs. Rottweiler, laughing at us and catching baseballs and throwing them at those God-awful geraniums like she didn't care anymore, and then the baseballs and the geraniums were gone and I was staring at her maplewood table, and the Planter's Peanut jar was back, and so were the dead pussy willows.

The very next thing I remember, and I didn't know time could blip by so fast, was me and my dad standing on the front steps of Mrs. Rottweiler's house and Winston Rottweiler opening the door and nodding and there was a grim, gray-haired look about his face even though he was the same age as my dad, and then the two of them were speaking in low, dry whispers so I couldn't catch what they were saying, and then we were inside. The place was pretty much cleaned out. The dirty, yellowish sofa and the roll-away t.v. were gone, and so was the white pine bookcase. The antique china cupboard and the maplewood table were still there, but the cupboard was empty, and the table was covered with boxes and stacks of letters on one half, and on the other half there was an old wind-up alarm clock and about a dozen dusty fruit jars with the lids missing and Mr. Rottweiler's old army duffel bag from before he died in the war, and a lot of other junk besides. The first thing Winston did when we were inside he gave my dad a hard clap on the shoulder and the two of them started talking some more, with Winston waving at the junk on the table and my dad nodding and then both of them almost laughing, and then they went off into the kitchen. I could barely hear them after that, but from time to time I did catch a few words about when they were kids and Mrs. Rottweiler was chasing after them, but mostly I wasn't interested, and then the sound of their voices drifted out through the back door.

I don't know exactly how long my dad planned on staying. It was kind of like he'd forgotten I was there. My dad was like that sometimes. He'd take you somewhere, and maybe you didn't even want to go there in the first place, and before you knew it you were on your own. Anyway, I started looking through one of the boxes on the table and it had a record player in it and some old records, and one of them was a Lawrence Welk record. It was called *Sweet and Lovely*. I took it out and looked at the picture of Mr. Welk in the upper corner. He was smiling, wearing a black jacket with just the white of his collar showing, and it looked to me like he wanted to dance, like he was done with his show and just about to ask some lady from the audience to dance the last dance with him, you could tell it by his smile, and I was thinking wouldn't it have been funny to see Mrs. Rottweiler in her housecoat with the peacocks dancing with Lawrence Welk, only as soon as I thought it, it didn't seem so much a joke, it seemed to me that the two times I'd seen her dancing, that was exactly what she'd been doing. I wondered if Mrs. Rottweiler dancing like that with Lawrence Welk bothered Mr. Rottweiler, even if he was dead, I mean you didn't know what he was thinking, up there for about thirty God-awful years and his wife dancing like she was with an old-fogey band leader. But maybe he didn't care. Then I was wondering if Mrs. Rottweiler had ever been to *The Lawrence Welk Show* in person, or if she had only just watched it on her roll-away t.v. I wondered if she had danced with Lawrence Welk in the flesh, or if it had always been in her mind. I don't know how long I stood there wondering like that, cause my mind sort of went blank after a while, and the next thing I knew I was running out Mrs. Rottweiler's front door with the record player and the Lawrence Welk record both. Just like with the baseballs. I can't tell you what I was thinking. I mean I wasn't too big on Lawrence Welk or anything like that. I was just standing there and then all of a sudden I could see Mrs. Rottweiler dancing with Lawrence Welk. I guess I went a little loony myself. But I couldn't get that image out of my mind.

The funeral was two days later, and the church was packed, which was saying something because our church was a big old gothic style church built of solid granite and oak beams, and it had twelve stained-glass windows about thirty feet high on each side. It was so big it seemed to swallow you up when you stepped inside, but it was packed for Mrs. Rottweiler. In the front pews there were about fifty little old ladies in their fluffy owl-feather hats and white tennies, and a few old geezers stuffed in between them, the old ladies rattling away on their Rosaries, and the old geezers just sitting there, looking stupidly at Mrs. Rottweiler's casket. Like cows or something. After that there was my dad and a whole bunch of neighbors, even some I didn't know, and then there was Jimmy Lundgren's dad, he had closed down the Meat Market from across the street to come, and I saw the Schultz brothers from the S & S Grocery and even Todd Schneider's dad from the Mobil on the other side of the highway. It looked like just about everybody had closed down for Mrs. Rottweiler. And behind all the grown-ups were the school kids. We always got out of school when there was a funeral and we'd sit in the back of the church and chew gum on the sly and shoot spit balls at each other, and mostly we didn't care if we could see the casket or not.

I still don't remember everything about that funeral. I don't remember the end of, that's one thing for sure. But when it began, there I was sitting up in the choir loft, and everybody else was down below. I was sitting in a chair up against the back wall and there was a small, scuffed-up end table next to me, and Mrs. Rottweiler's old record player was on the table. I was holding the Lawrence Welk record in my hand. At first I just sat there and listened to the priest talking, mumbling was more like it, and then there was a silence, which I was sure Mrs. Rottweiler didn't want, so I plugged in the record player and put on the record and cranked the knob as loud as it would go. You wouldn't have believed what happened next. I was kneeling up at the rail, looking down, and it was like everybody was frozen, some were looking up at the choir loft, their faces twisted in pain like they'd been hit in the stomach with a baseball bat, especially Mrs. Phillips, she looked like probably two baseball bats had got her, but the rest were looking directly at Mrs. Rottweiler's casket, or just about three feet above it, which was where I was looking, and there was Mrs. Rottweiler herself, dressed in her housecoat with the flapping, dancing peacocks and her white tennies and her nylon stockings falling down around her ankles, but she wasn't old, it was like she was a young girl all over again, and she was dancing to the music, the same little polka steps from before, but she was young again, and what was more, Lawrence Welk was dancing right there with her. They were dancing there above the casket and the hazy morning sunlight streaming in through the stained-glass windows was all around them, and Mr. Welk was smiling and saying something to Mrs. Rottweiler and then she was almost smiling and humming to the music, and her eyes were half-closed all the while she was humming, and then you couldn't see them for a moment, because of the sunlight, and then you could, and then the music was over, like someone had suddenly snapped it off, but by then it didn't really matter because Mrs. Rottweiler and Lawrence Welk had already danced themselves out through one of the stained-glass windows.

The Lingering Death of Eamon Patterson

Eamon Patterson and his wife, Leila, lived in a small nameless, mostly Catholic town along the Gulf Coast, a town which smelled of paper mills and pine and burning tar and river sewage when the wind came from the north, and salt water and old beer and rotting fish and motor oil when the wind came from the south, and which, perhaps because of the thought-provoking quality of so many distinct yet native odors blended together, boasted the fewest occupants of any town in the county, twenty-two people and thirteen itinerant dogs, and with the exception of the dogs, and one or possibly two people, if you counted both Pattersons, everyone had been expecting Eamon Patterson to die for the last thirty years.

The town itself was in the last stages of its abandonment and it seemed more a symbol of municipal oblivion than anything else. There were four or five white clapboard houses in town and a few more outside the limits, and a Standard Oil with one pump working and two pumps not working down along the Old Kings Highway, and they sold Cokes there and Ne-Hi Orange and peanuts and chewing gum and even some Dolly Cakes when they weren't selling any gas, which was most of the time. The only store within the town limits was McCabe's Drugstore, which masqueraded as a church on Sundays and the Post Office on Tuesday mornings, and across from McCabe's was an old abandoned movie house, which some had thought a disgrace when it first went out of business and wanted to tear it down for the vanity fixtures, they were made of pink and white marble and suggested the extravagance of New York City or Boston or some such place, but the Widow Mrs. J. D. Dobbs, she was the only Protestant in town, said they couldn't do that, the building was historic, a landmark, and then she turned it into a Christian mission and hung out a sign and had soup and sandwiches five days a week and Bible readings every other night. It was for the vagrants she said, any that came this way, though there weren't but a handful ever showed up at any one time, and they seemed to come mostly for the free soup. Eamon couldn't have a picked a more appropriate town to die in.

The death of Eamon began the day an ancient traveling miracle man came to town to do a show. The man arrived in a dilapidated milk truck, it still had the word **"MILK"** printed on both sides in a neat arc, but he did look vaguely Spanish, which suggested to the townspeople great passion, and perhaps even violence, and since such idiosyncrasies were a rarity in this town, at least as part of a public spectacle, there was a crowd of maybe a dozen who came simply to watch the ancient miracle man set up his platform stage in the sandy, grassy lot next to the abandoned movie house. They watched with a deliberate and yet humble interest, even the dogs. And everything the man brought out spoke marvels. On one side there was a table displaying a variety of oddly shaped musical instruments and a collection of antique weapons, mostly swords edged with rust, but there was also a small boot-strap derringer, which the miracle man waved at the watchers and said it was the gun Jesse James had been killed with and then he set it down. On the other side there was a mysterious trunk with strange, arcane scribblings on it and pictures of the sun and the moon and the stars and a man poling a long boat in a sea of fish and a woman with the head of a baboon, all of which the miracle man claimed was a fair example of Egyptian writing. Then, since there was nothing more to be done about the stage, the ancient miracle man put out a sign which said the next show was at one o'clock and disappeared into the back of his truck. Then the people began to talk.

"What does it mean there the next show is at one o'clock? He aint even done the first show yet."

"Maybe he's only got one sign."

"Who'd this fellow say he was?"

"He didn't say."

"Well I aint gonna watch him less I know who he is."

"What are you talking about Hubert. You'd watch him if it was raining whether you knew him or not. So would the rest of us."

"Would not."

"I heard he came all the way from St. Louis. I got a cousin over in One-Egg and she saw him a couple of weeks ago. That's what she said."

"What'd he come down here for?"

"I don't know. That's just what I heard."

"Your cousin have an opinion about the show?"

"No. She pretty much keeps her mind to herself. But she did say they ran him off after three or four days."

"That's good enough for me."

And then it was one o'clock, and from the moment the ancient miracle man began his routine, the entire town, except for Eamon Patterson, who had fallen asleep after a lunch of cold crabmeat and crackers and a piece of store-bought pie, but including the various mongrel and pedigreed dogs, which in this time of the almost mythic past numbered twenty-seven, they all fell into a feverish almost clownish trance, the people clapping their hands, and the dogs dancing. Then the miracle man called out for volunteers and the clapping and dancing stopped and two men scrambled onto the stage, and also a young girl, and the miracle man gave them each an instrument and then instructed them how to play, and then he smiled and said he had never had a pupil fail him yet, though it seemed a certainty this time, for the two men were swinging their instruments about as they might wrenches, and the girl was tone deaf. Then the miracle man commanded his less than musically inclined trio to play, and they did, and what's more it sounded like something you could hear on the radio, which some said it was – they were sure there was a radio somewhere in the back of that milk truck, and one even tried to get in and see – but the rest said it was a mystery only God could explain. Even the Widow Mrs. Dobbs was impressed, and she later said that the giddy, unrehearsed virtuosity of the performance was more than enough to make a body convert on the spot, though just what she'd have been converting to she didn't say. Then everybody clapped some more and the trio left the stage, and then the miracle man launched into a recitation of some passage, from Homer, he said, from a long long poem called *The Iliad*, and he was going to do it in the original Latin first and then explain it afterwards, which he did, and everyone said it was powerfully delivered and moving and very beautiful for poetry, but nobody understood it even after the explanation. Then he did a little play about the Wild West and bandied about the stage for a while with a sword in one hand and the derringer in the other, and it seemed well-acted, but it was hard to tell just what was going on, there being six or seven parts and only one actor, and when he was done with that he sang a couple of songs he said were love songs, and then he bowed to the women and saluted the men. Then he stood up and looked to his audience with fiercely dark eyes, Spanish eyes people would later say, and some of the women had to fan themselves in the heat of his glare, and some of the men wondered if there might be a fight. And some of the dogs too.

Then the miracle man made his pitch.

"My good, good people, let me direct your attention to the large trunk on my left. It is covered top to bottom with ancient Egyptian writing, hieroglyphics, as they say in the ivory towers of academia, and it contains The *Blue Elixir of the Nile*, a potion which, I don't mind telling you, can cure everything from cataracts to the common cold. But do not simply take my word for it." And then he moved over to the trunk and pulled out a drawer and picked up a handful of papers and waved them about. "These are signed affidavits from people like yourselves from here all the way to St. Louis. Signed in the presence of notaries and priests. But not even this, good people, not even the mighty weight of all this sworn testimony should persuade you to buy a bottle against your better judgement. What you need is actual proof, not paper." And then the miracle man tossed the sworn affidavits to the ground with a tremendous and practiced flourish. "What you need to do, good people, you need to witness the miracle of this blue elixir for yourselves. And only after you have been convinced of its curative properties should you buy a bottle for your very own."

The crowd murmured a furious amen, for they took what the ancient miracle man said to be a sort of New Deal gospel, and then he asked if any of them suffered from headaches or insomnia or boils or any one of a thousand and one ailments, and there was a flurry of nods, and then from out of the flurry the miracle man invited a young boy of about seventeen to come up and give the elixir a try. The boy's particular malady was marked by sporadic coughing and a graceless, stoop-shouldered gait, which most of the townspeople would have said was a sign the boy had taken up smoking or become a shiftless vagrant had not his sickness been generally acknowledged. Then the miracle man held up a bottle of blue elixir, a bottle which he had specially prepared the night before and which contained five parts grain alcohol and two parts blue elixir, and he gave the boy a swig and the boy gasped and stumbled to the edge of the stage and then fell headfirst onto the sandy, grassy ground, and when the people rolled him over and saw the twisted yet somehow joyously angelic smile spread across his face, the boy looked like a saint, they were suddenly and passionately convinced that the boy would never again suffer from his strange, graceless malady, a revelation which they pondered with a suitable amount of reverent awe, and then they turned towards the stage en masse and waved their arms wildly in the air and clamored almost desperately for as many bottles as the ancient miracle man could spare, and he in turn pulled bottle after blue bottle from out of the mysteriously inscribed trunk and sold them for three dollars a piece, which was more than usual, a good drunk was rarely worth more than a dollar, but then the ancient miracle man hadn't anticipated the sanctifying effect his potion would have on the vagrant boy.

It was then that Eamon Patterson arrived. He had fallen asleep in an old soft chair he kept out on the back porch, a pair of heavy work boots on the rough floor beneath, but then the timely stench of a south wind roused him from his stupor and he put on his boots and walked into town. He had sensed that something peculiar was taking place even a mile away, but what he saw when he stood in front of McCabe's drugstore he could hardly believe. The men were guzzling from tiny blue bottles and laughing and spitting out streams of blue liquid, and some were wrestling on the ground, and the women were saving their bottles for later but they were laughing as well, and some were even turning pirouettes in the street like music-box ballerinas. Even the dogs took part, following after the men, slipping in and out of legs, lapping at the puddles where the men had spit.   Then the two men and the young girl who had volunteered for the musical portion of the show once again grabbed instruments and began playing, and though they certainly fell short of the radio-style sound they had achieved earlier, nobody seemed to mind, not even the dogs, for they were all of them drunk with the maddening prospect of imminent salvation.

At first Eamon thought he was still asleep, for even the sunlight burned with the heat of a dream, but gradually he came to understand that the town was possessed of a great madness, even his wife seemed overwhelmed, she was in front of the movie house-mission dancing with a Cocker Spaniel. And then Eamon saw the ancient miracle man, the dark complexion, the fiercely dark eyes, an impatient vendor of obscure reputation who had just shoved the last of this town's legal tender into a large, brown burlap sack and was ready to dismantle the stage and load up the milk wagon, and the instant Eamon looked at the man and saw the sack he felt within himself a deep and burgeoning rage, he would not let this vagabond quack of a thief work over the town, he had to do something, and in the novelty of this sudden heroism, for he had never had such feelings before, he charged towards the sandy, grassy lot and the drinking, dancing people, and all the while he was waving his arms in the air and shouting almost incoherently about wrack and ruin.

Immediately the dancing and drinking stopped, and the people fanned out to let Eamon pass, the dogs too, but as Eamon neared the stage he slowed and then stopped, for he wasn't sure what to do next. The miracle man, for his part, had looked suddenly less miraculous during the charge, but in the absence of any continued movement from Eamon he regained his color, and then he began to mock Eamon's stationary ambivalence with a wink to the crowd and a cavalier laugh. Of course by this time the crowd had become somewhat suspicious of this miracle man with a large burlap sack in his hand, for in their memory Eamon had never been one to act so impetuously, and so they looked at the sack and then they looked at the bottles they were holding and then again at the sack, and then suddenly the imagined effect of the blue elixir was gone, and the crowd surged past the still stationary and now seemingly perplexed Eamon Patterson and demanded their money back, and then receiving no answer, for the ancient miracle man was now behind the wheel of his dilapidated milk truck and driving away, they hurled empty and half-empty and even full bottles of this *Blue Elixir of the Nile* at the receding truck, some of the bottles breaking against the two flapping back doors and all sorts of theatrical paraphernalia spilling out, and some of the bottles landing among the splintered remnants of the stage, for it had been loosely fixed to the back of the truck and unable to withstand the torque of so hasty an exit.

Then the barrage stopped, for the people had no bottles left, and anyway, the ancient miracle man and his milk truck were beyond their immediate reach, they didn't think about pursuit, and so in the frustration of their rage they turned upon the spilled-out heap of musical instruments and antique weapons (the swords and a few muskets, but not the derringer) and a few brightly colored costumes, and in the middle of the heap sat the mysteriously inscribed trunk, its many drawers now on the ground and affidavits scattered about, and also dozens and dozens of pharmaceutical company catalogues. At first all the townspeople did was throw things around and shout and stamp their feet and say God damn it and that was all the money they had and they'd show him he ever showed his face in this town again, and then they thought to make a great a pile of everything the miracle man had abandoned, which they did, and some were for having a sale and some were for burning it and the Widow Mrs. Dobbs was for giving it away, but they just couldn't agree on what was best for the town. Then all of sudden they heard a great shout, or a gunshot, or perhaps it was the sound of a motor backfiring, for when they turned they saw the ancient miracle man driving his dilapidated milk truck towards them in a jerky but slow-moving kind of frenzy, and then the truck stopped and the miracle man climbed out. He had the boot-strap derringer in his hand, and in the dream of his return he pointed the small pistol directly at Eamon, who ever since his heroic but aborted charge had remained in a kind of daze. Nobody moved.

Then the miracle man spoke.

"You there. You have dared to rouse the suspicions of these good, good people against me, and falsely so. I should kill you now. But there is no need. In three days you will begin to die, and your death will be a lingering death, so that everyone here will know it comes from your own iniquity and not some natural cause."

So the ancient miracle man climbed into his milk truck and drove away, and the townspeople watched him go, and so did Eamon Patterson, and then the everyone began to go home in two's and three's, though not without a few sideways almost fearful glances at the man who was to die a lingering death, for these were people who believed in curses.

Three days later, Eamon and the town's only doctor were playing a game of checkers on the Patterson's back porch. The doctor had decided to pay a call on account of this curse of the lingering death, he too was a firm believer, and so Eamon had invited him in and Leila fixed them both turkey sandwiches and some iced tea and there they were. They had been playing for some time, and had, in fact, quite forgotten about the curse in the obsession of their thirty-ninth game, when Eamon suddenly doubled over on top of the checkerboard and fell to the floor, the checker pieces scattering about the room. At first the doctor did nothing, for he suddenly wondered if the curse were contagious, but then he heard Leila step onto the porch and gasp. She almost knocked the good doctor over in her haste to reach her heap of a husband. Then the two of them dragged Eamon's unconscious body into the house, the doctor pulling Eamon by the ankles in his efforts to steer clear of contagion, and Leila holding up one arm as best she could to keep her husband's fat head from banging against the floor.

"You must save him, doctor."

"I'll do what I can."

"Will that be enough?"

"I don't know. I'm not all that knowledgeable when it comes to curses."

They dumped Eamon in the good mahogany bed and pulled off his boots and the doctor said maybe they could draw the sickness out with a mustard plaster, and so he sent Leila to the kitchen to mix it up, but when she returned with the paste, the doctor had seemingly given up. He was hunched over in the mahogany chair next to the bed, his eyes fixed on the pale, motionless features of Eamon's face, and he seemed to be mumbling to himself. He gave no sign that he had heard Leila come in, she was standing but three steps behind him, but then he turned suddenly and spoke to her.

"It's no use. He's dying for sure."

"No. He's not dying. You said you would help him."

"I know what I said. But it's no use. There's nothing I can do. This is no ordinary sickness."

"But what about the plaster?"

Then the doctor relented and took the bowl from Leila's hands and applied a thin coat of paste to Eamon's skin, and then some gauze to keep in the heat, the doctor always kept a roll in his coat pocket for emergencies, and then he was finished and he said the best thing would be to leave Eamon alone give the plaster a chance to work yes that would be best let him sleep through the night and she should lock the door this was no ordinary sickness there was no telling what Eamon might do in his delirium he was sure of that, and then the doctor smiled at Leila and they left the empty bowl at the foot of the bed, and Eamon to the lingering of his death.

By noon the following day, everyone who had flung a bottle at the ancient miracle man, which was everyone in town, had shown up at the Patterson doorstep, some with hot tuna casseroles in hand, some with sandwiches and beer, some with fresh baked pies, and some with baskets of fruit and nuts. Everyone behaved as if Eamon were already dead, which meant they were bothered by guilt, for in the confusion of their accumulated superstitions, they now believed that each bottle of this *Blue Elixir of the Nile* meant life and each broken bottle meant death, and since the town had broken every bottle, Eamon's death was a foregone conclusion. It was as if the town itself had delivered the curse, not the miracle man, and so the townspeople sought a reconciliation of sorts, if not with Eamon, for he remained in a semicomatose state behind the locked bedroom door, then perhaps with Leila. They spent the next two hours eating and drinking and attesting to the apparent virtues of the one who had been cursed, and some not so apparent, and it was all Leila could do not to cry.

"Eamon he sure was a good old boy."

"You're telling me. I remember when Eamon and Leila first came to town. They didn't know nobody and nobody seemed interested in knowing them, and then a couple days later Eamon he came into the Standard Oil and started telling jokes and then he bought everybody a Coke. He was always doing something like that. Ask my wife."

Then a murmur of masculine agreement, a few hands reaching for some more sandwiches, some more beer, and then a few quick looks across the hall at the women in the dining room, the women sitting in the good dining room chairs, the curtains drawn out of respect for the dead, or almost dead, a small, dark circle in the dimly lit room, the women in a conversation of their own, more refined, elegant, almost subdued.

"Well all I know is there was nothing that poor old Eamon wouldn't do. Why if the rest of them louts sitting over there were half as considerate there wouldn't be a single one of us have to worry about going into debt or getting to Sunday church on time."

"You remember how he used to take Leila to town on Saturday afternoons?"

"I sure do."

"The two of them arm in arm and looking for all the world like they were going to a ball."

"And if she wanted something like a new hat or one of them fancy, ivory-handled New York umbrellas, he'd march her straight into McCabe's and order her one then and there right out of the Sears catalogue."

"Now there was a man knew how to treat a woman."

Then the women thinking about umbrellas or hats. And then the men again.

"And he was one hell of a checker player, wasn't he?"

"I never seen anything like it."

"I don't think I ever beat him but once in my life."

"You were lucky. I must have played him a thousand times and damn if he didn't beat me every single time."

"I think he'd rather of been playing checkers than just about anything else. No offense to Leila. But that board was always up."

"Well one thing's for sure, he must have died happy. I mean one minute he was thinking checkers and happy as a dog and the next he just keeled over."

"He was sure lucky."

"He sure was."

Then there was nothing more to say about the good man Eamon once was, and so the women began clearing away dishes and washing them and wiping down the good table and the side tables, and all the while humming, it sounded a little like hymns, all except Leila, who by this time was sleeping in the old soft chair on the back porch. As for the men, one of them said he couldn't think of a better way to honor their collective memory of Eamon than to have themselves a checker tournament, and so they set up half a dozen checker boards in the front room. (Eamon kept a ready supply in the front hall closet for all sorts of get-togethers in spite of his wife's insistence that being social was more than sitting around the house jumping for kings.)

But before even one piece had been played, Eamon himself appeared at the top of the stairs.

Of course no one knew what to think, except for a vague "that looks like Eamon," and all they could do was look up in awe at this apparition of their disbelief. What they saw was a man who looked to be asleep wearing nothing but boxer shorts and some thin white socks, and he was holding a large bowl on his hip but it was empty, and his skin was a mustardy yellow color, except where the gauze was still stuck, and he even smelled like mustard, it was a strong smell which carried down the steps and then into the various rooms on the first floor, and even years later when people came by to visit they would often remark that the whole house smelled like mustard, especially if it was their first time. Then the doctor stood up and faced the gawking incredulity before him and with a rigid composure born of professional discipline, as well as a stubborn though understandable desire to live to be one-hundred years old, he told them it was not a ghost, at least not yet, but they were in mortal danger nevertheless, for Eamon's sickness of the lingering death was quite possibly contagious, like cholera or bubonic plague, and until they knew for certain, meaning they should keep an eye on Leila for a couple of weeks and see if she came down with anything, they'd best give Eamon as wide a berth as was possible in a small town. The men murmured in grim and uncertain agreement, for they had yet to satisfy themselves that Eamon was truly among the not-dead, and then one went to warn the women, and the rest weaved their way out past the readied checker boards and the empty beer bottles, the doctor too. A few minutes later the house was empty, save for Leila on the porch, and Eamon at the top of the stairs, and they were both still asleep.

When Eamon woke the next morning he found himself in the soft chair on the porch, and at first it seemed to him that only a moment had passed since he and the good doctor had been playing checkers, that his sickness was not a sickness at all but something he had imagined, but then he saw the checker board on the floor, and also a few pieces, and he knew this wasn't so. "I am dying," he said to himself. And then he looked out through the screened-in porch and all around him was death. There was the fig tree in the sandy, grassy yard, and he remembered eating the figs, he and Leila would pick them on summer evenings and then sit on the porch and eat them and laugh and talk and sometimes Leila would sing and he would listen, and sometimes they would hear the far away basset horn sound of the ships calling to each other out on the Gulf and they would both listen, but there weren't as many figs this year as in years past, which suggested to Eamon then and there that the fig tree was dying a lingering death of its own. Then there was the smell of dead fish and dead crabs and the sour wet smells of the packing plants rising up from the south, and beyond that there was the smell of disinfectant. And from high up in the pines he heard a blue jay shriek, and even this sounded like death. Then Eamon called out to Leila, for he did not want to die alone, but she was slicing fruit in the kitchen and singing softly the same hymns the other women had sung the day before and did not hear him. Then he thought about the miracle man and the blue elixir, and he wished he had come with the others and bought a bottle instead of coming late and charging the stage, and then it occurred to him that if he had a bottle of his own he might not die, and then he was sure this was so, and in this glare of sudden insight he looked down at the floor and there in a heap next to his boots he saw dozens and dozens of pharmaceutical company catalogues, the very same catalogues that had spilled out of the miracle man's trunk upon his hasty, first departure, and without stopping even to consider how the catalogues had appeared – Eamon simply assumed that it was somehow God's doing, which meant he should send off for a bottle of this *Blue Elixir of the Nile* right away – he plucked the first catalogue from the floor and began paging through it. When Leila brought out a bowl of cut fruit for his breakfast he didn't even notice.

The catalogues became for Eamon an obsession. Once a week, most often after church on Sunday, for then he would be suitably inspired, he would sift through them until he came up with a list of three or four up till then uncontacted companies and then he would write three or four letters explaining about the curse and his lingering death and his need for this miraculous elixir and would they please send him a bottle. He spent hours writing these letters, sometimes far into the night, a fat, desperate figure wedged into a wicker chair on the porch of his insomnia, a stack of empty white paper on one corner of a small writing table, the faint, flickering yellow light of a kerosene lamp hanging from a hook, the heavy dark blue of the night pressing in against the screens and the hum of mosquitos, and no two letters were exactly the same, for Eamon felt he never quite captured the sense of urgency his unconventional sickness demanded, and so he was constantly reworking his thoughts, a detail here, there, maybe he should put in the part about the boot-strap derringer, and there it would be in the next letter, and then all of the letters would be written and stuffed into their envelopes (even though Eamon was never satisfied, he did not waste paper), and a few dollars besides to cover the cost of the elixir. Then he would check off the names of the three or four companies and shove the catalogues underneath the table and put himself to bed.

The next thing he knew it would be late Tuesday morning around eleven o'clock, Monday's seemed to slide by unnoticed, and Eamon would slip the letters into his shirt pocket and head off to McCabe's to see if there were any word yet or a package and drop the new batch in the mail if there weren't, and sometimes he'd sit a while and talk politics and have a Coke, and sometimes he wouldn't. It took him several months to go through the catalogues the first time, and then he went through them a second time, and a third, and then he lost track. He lived in the void of infinite expectation, for every time he walked into McCabe's he imagined himself opening a small brown package and then pulling out a palm-sized bottle of the almost certainly by then mythical blue elixir and offering it up to McCabe and anyone else who happened to be in the drugstore as proof that he wasn't as mad as people had started to say. For thirty years Eamon went to McCabe's, and the absence of even a letter in all that time never discouraged him. Nor did the practical but passionate wisdom of Mr. McCabe.

"Aint nothing come in for you this week, Eamon."

"I can see that myself."

"You got some more letters you want sent out?"

"These three."

"Eamon, I don't know why you're wasting all this paper. Them companies they aint never gonna send you a bottle. Hell, Eamon, how they gonna send you something you living in a town aint even got a name."

"You just wait and see. This is God's doing we're talking about. One of these days there's gonna be a small, brown package in that there cubby and you'll see."

"Well, maybe you're right Eamon. But all the same I wouldn't be too confident. Like as not the stuff in that bottle you're looking for don't exist no more. They'll probably go send you the wrong damn thing."

"Nothing I can do about that. But you'll see."

"I suppose I will at that. See you next week, Eamon."

"Be seeing you."

And then Eamon would head for home with his unsuspecting faith like that of a dog and his mind already writing and rewriting a new batch of letters. He believed in the hand of God. But what he didn't know was that for as long as he had been sending his letters and drinking Cokes at McCabe's and waiting for that small, brown package to arrive in the dream of his cubbyhole, his wife, Leila, had been intercepting the post and burying whatever came in a great jagged hole in back of Henderson's junkyard some fifteen yards from the black Fishweir river. Of course Leila also believed in the hand of God, but she was never so vocal as Eamon, and in this time of the curse her silent faith became an elusive thing and was immediately replaced by the harsh, imposing voice and apocalyptic presence of the doctor. The very day Eamon had gone to McCabe's with his first batch of letters, within ten minutes of his handing them over, the good and ever vigilant doctor had come knocking on the Patterson front door and was soon instructing poor Leila on the folly of Eamon's endeavor.

"This letter writing is not a good thing, Leila."

"But he only just started."

"Yes. I know. I know. But the moment one of those pharmaceutical companies writes back and tells poor Eamon there is no elixir – and they will tell him this truth, Leila, you mark my words – what do you think will happen then? No, no. The shock and disappointment would be too much for him. He'd be dead within minutes."

"What can we do?"

"The only thing we can. You must go to McCabe's every Tuesday morning. Before Eamon. And any letters that come you must burn them. Every Tuesday, Leila. And Eamon must never, ever know. This is no ordinary sickness. We wouldn't want to make things any worse."

She did what was asked, except she buried the letters instead of burning them, for she was not as decisive as the doctor, and besides, the letters terrified her, they were like dead things, like Eamon would be if he read them, and you did not burn dead things in this nameless, Catholic town, you put them in the earth. And so every Tuesday she would wake up an hour or so before Eamon and hurry to the make-shift Post Office, and sometimes the door would be locked when she got there, so she'd sit herself on the greenish, wrought-iron bench out front and hum to herself some song from the radio and watch the morning doves twittering in the sunny, dusty, warming street, and then they would fly away, and sometimes McCabe would be working behind the counter, a small brass lamp turned on, the faint glow of an electric bulb almost lost in the morning blue shadows of the empty storeroom, and Leila would wait on the bench outside or on one of the stools by the counter until McCabe had sorted the mail, and if there was anything for Eamon he would wrap the letters in a rag of blue oilcloth and lay the bundle up by the register, and if there wasn't he would disappear into the back without so much as a grunt, and on those days when there was something, Leila would pick up the bundle and head on down to the black black Fishweir river and her place of concealment in back of Henderson's junkyard, and in the haze of her burden she would shovel away the dirt from the time before, there was always a shovel, though how it came to be there she did not know, and then she would toss the bundle into the hole and cover it up again. She never read the letters. She didn't dare.

And she always made it home in time to fix Eamon his lunch. And Eamon would always come in with that smile of a happy dog and sit down in the old soft chair on the porch and eat his turkey or tuna or crabmeat sandwiches and a couple of Cokes, and then a thick slab of store-bought pie. He never even saw the dirt beneath her fingernails.

The only other person who knew about the buried letters was McCabe, for Leila had told no one in the terror of the doctor's advice. The doctor himself seemed little interested in the fate of Eamon and the letters after that first week, or in Leila either, for he had never gotten over his first impulse that this curse of the lingering death was contagious, and so in time he made himself quite absent from the Patterson household, and he rarely came within fifteen feet if he saw them in town. As for McCabe, he was relentless in his silence, for he believed that what people did was their own business, particularly if those people were married, and yet he also believed in the integrity of Leila's intentions, he could see it in her face when she walked into his store or waited outside on the bench, this love of enduring despair, and so he had helped her from the beginning. It was McCabe who had taken her to the loamy, bare patch in back of the junkyard and started her digging. It was McCabe who had provided the shovel. And if she failed to thank him, or even acknowledge his grandfatherly role in this conspiracy of the pharmaceutical company letters, as McCabe had come to think of it, it was only because she, too, had become a victim of the miracle man's curse.

Only Eamon was more alone.

And then it was thirty years to the day since the miracle man had set up his show and sold his blue bottles. It was also a Tuesday, and Leila was in back of the junkyard, only she was having a tough time digging because it had rained heavily the night before and the dirt was a sticky, clumpy, muddy mass, and every time she pushed the shovel into the ground it seemed like she was sinking into a deep, watery grave, which frightened her, and it was hard to pull the shovel out against the strength of this grave, as if a corpse were holding onto the shovel from below and would not let go, but then there would be a slow, sharp, sucking sound, and then she would slop a shovelful to the ground behind her and dig some more. There were two thick bundles of letters this time, which she had left in the damp, weedy grass by the junkyard fence while she dug the hole, and also a small, brown paper package about the size of a pack of cigarettes, which she had put in the front pocket of her petticoat, and she was thinking she wasn't going to finish the hole it was taking too long it was almost time for Eamon to have his lunch but then what was she going to do with all this mail, but she never had the chance to answer her own, unspoken question, for in the moment of her desperation she heard the voice of McCabe, it seemed to hover in the air directly above the black, watery hole that was not yet deep enough, and the voice simply said, "It's Eamon." Leila turned to see the back of the darkly dressed McCabe climbing up around the corner of the junkyard fence, the shoulder and arm of a dark green shirt, the squared heel of one black boot, and then she climbed up after him.

The next thing Leila knew she was standing in her own front yard, though she didn't seem too sure about this, and even looked to the large and thickly brooding McCabe standing next to her, she was almost clutching his arm, for some sign of confirmation, but McCabe said nothing. Leila was sure she was dreaming. There were dogs everywhere, thirteen of them, some scratching at the bushes by the steps, some looking up at the second story bedroom window where Eamon was and then a few low, moaning sounds from their throats and then moving off, and a couple even looked like they were dead themselves the way they were stretched out in the sandy grass, and they smelled like they were dead, too, dead or dying. And then there were the people, everyone was there, and some were standing about in two's and three's in the spitting heat of twelve o'clock, never in all her life had Leila felt such a sun as this, as if she were drowning in heat, a strange orange sun like a great sea spitting waves of heat, and some others were squatting down in the thick but warm shade of the front stoop or sitting bent-kneed on the rail and staring at the dogs, and the people did not move in the orange glare of Leila's confusion, but at the same time they spoke in low, desiccated murmurs, it sure took him a long long time, poor Eamon have a curse like that laying on his head and for thirty years too, I feel sorry for the man, I do too, but all the same it's too bad it couldn't of happened sooner, I tell you what if that miracle man show up again he gonna have a lot of explaining to do a lot of explaining, I don't mean no disrespect to the dead but you look at Leila now, I'd forgotten all about that miracle man show, what's she gonna do, and them bottles too, she's too old to start over and too young to give up herself where's she gonna go, why I'd give anything have one of them blue bottles right now, why if Eamon had died even ten years ago Leila could of found herself another husband but now there aint nobody left, what was that he called it, it's just too bad all the way around, that's right, *The Blue Elixir of the Nile*, that's right, it's just too, too bad.

Then the voices stopped, and Leila and McCabe went up the steps and inside, and the house was strangely dark, a heavy purple dark, as if it were already a place of shadows, but not a single curtain was drawn, for in the revelation of Eamon's first collapse, Leila had removed every curtain from the house, as if by doing so she could prevent his death from coming. So the orange sun raged against the uncurtained windows with the same feverish, orange glow as on the unmoving people and the thirteen dogs outside, but in the house it was still dark. Then the doctor appeared in the hall and ushered them into the dying room, and he said there was nothing he could do this time he wasn't a priest, and then he smiled weakly at Leila and left. Leila said nothing for a moment, and then she edged her way over to the bed and to Eamon and sat down, but Eamon did not recognize her. She closed her eyes and thought about Eamon now dying and what was she going to do and what

was wrong with that doctor, and then she thought maybe to
say a small prayer, but in the blur of her distress she
couldn't remember one, and then she took a single, deep
breath and opened her eyes, and there was her Eamon
sitting up in bed, and he had in his hands a small, brown
package. Instinctively, Leila reached for her pocket, but of
course it was empty now, but whether she had taken it out
herself or he had she did not know. Then Eamon opened
the package and took out a small, blue bottle with a label
that said *The Blue Elixir of the Nile* in fancy script, and
then suddenly in this dream of his death Eamon saw himself
standing across from the miracle man's stage and the
abandoned movie house and he tried to call out, he tried to
stop his former self from charging the drinking, dancing
crowd and that thief of a miracle man who was maybe not
a thief, but then there he was waving his arms in the air and
shouting about wrack and ruin, and then just as suddenly
the crowd was gone, and so was the miracle man, and all he
had was the bottle in his hands. Then he looked to his wife
and showed her the bottle, and then he saw McCabe
brooding in the heavy purplish shadows of the far corner
and held it up so he could see too, and then he spoke,
though even Leila did not see his mouth move.

"I told you all it would come. I told you. This here is
God's doing."

Then Eamon Patterson unscrewed the cap to the small
bottle and nodded in the direction of Leila, and then
McCabe, and before either could say a word he poured this

Blue Elixir of the Nile down his throat, and then he gasped, and then he died.

They buried him that afternoon, of course, for death by curse was an unusual kind of death, and also unsettling, in case it became an epidemic, and so the townspeople wanted to be done with the whole affair as quickly as possible. They did not, however, bury Eamon in the cemetery lot, for the doctor, still cautious about the possibility of contagion, suggested a more remote site, and though Leila protested, the good doctor carried the town, for he still had about him an apocalyptic presence. Instead, they buried Eamon in the same jagged hole which contained the many letters he had received over the years, and when Leila died a few months later, they dug another hole not two feet from the first and buried her in this second grave of her enduring love. In time, of course, the curse was forgotten, and then one by one, the rest of the townspeople either died or moved away, the dogs, too, until only the ever-vigilant doctor was left. He himself was unaware of his abandonment and spent several hours each day calling on imaginary patients and treating their every ill with an imaginary roll of gauze, for he had long since run out. And then one warm, dark, rainy afternoon, the good doctor died, just three days after his one-hundredth birthday, and in the fever of this last, lingering death, the ancient miracle man returned once more. He buried the doctor next to Eamon and his wife, and then he climbed back into his dilapidated milk truck and drove away, slowly motoring towards the rain-drenched coast.

Love's Baby Gone East of the Redneck Riviera

What Marion Gunner wanted most when he came home after work was a nice cold beer, a quiet dark place by the window, where he could sit and look out from his garage apartment at the narrow evening-blue wedge of the street below, the drowsy hum of a few soft-burning street lamps, a few late model cars parked in front of dirty, clapboard houses, maybe catch a glimpse of one of those teenage prostitutes in a black, clingy-knit dress with black high heels heading for the brown stucco down the block, and most of all, though more because it had become a habit than anything else, what he wanted was the absence of his wife. On most evenings this is precisely what he got, but on this particular Floridian summer evening, with its thick, penetrating, swarming, moist heat, and its hazy, heavy dark, there was no cold beer waiting, no quiet place by the window, and Marion Gunner's wife was sitting at the bottom of the unpainted stairs.

She looked up as he pulled into the driveway, her coarsely scrubbed, whitish face becoming desperately, almost aggressively eager, and his rusted, blue Pontiac skidded to a stop, but he, in spite of his beer-driven thirst, did not immediately get out of the car. He sat there a moment, regarding his wife with a mixture of suspicion and bewilderment, for he was as startled by her presence as if he had begun to shed his own skin. With sudden, agitated steps she traced her way around to the driver's side, passing in front of the grill. She could feel the heaving, still shuddering, peeling-off heat of the engine, and in the timid confusion of her resolve, for she had not approached her young husband like this in several months, she thought of it as coming from him instead. The twitching of her hips as she spoke kept him in his seat.

"You feel like going somewhere?" she said.

"No I don't. I been somewhere already."

"Well I do," she said. "It's God awful hot up there. Too hot. I turned out the lights. But that didn't help. Feels like the whole place is melting straight on down to the floor. C'mon, Gunner. Let's go somewhere. Somewhere cool."

He didn't say anything, bent his head half-drowsily against the steering wheel, but kept his eyes on her hips, still twitching. She waited. They heard the clinking of bottles followed by low, husky laughter, and she looked up at the dark, screen-heavy shadow of the garage apartment, and so did he, but the sounds were distorted, swollen, they seemed to envelop the entire neighborhood, so just where they came from was impossible to say. But she knew. That afternoon her stepbrother, Robey, and his wife and their three runty, red-haired boys had wandered up the drive, their clothes patched with odd bits of cloth and streaked with grease and sweat and road-dust, their eyes and faces swollen from the spitting heat of the sun. Mr. Guernsey, who lived in the bungalow next door, and had been living there most of his eighty years, had come out and tried to chase them away, calling them hoodlums and vandals and worse and he was going to call the police if they didn't leave, what business did they have there anyway, so Robey had told him, and Mr. Guernsey had gone back inside.

At first Suzanne had simply stood at the door, unable to say a word, and they, too, stood wordlessly on the other side, eyes blinking solemnly, sluggishly. Slowly then, faintly perspiring, her face twisted into a half-smile of apology, she had opened the door, and her stepbrother had mumbled a grim, fatigued, tight-lipped thanks, and he and his taciturn brood had settled into the apartment, as dust settles. Hearing the bottles and the husky laughter now she blanched. She had told Robey it would take some doing, she'd have to get Marion away from the apartment and get him drunk, and even then she couldn't promise more than a couple of nights. Good God, why her husband didn't even know she had a stepbrother, much less one out of work and a family to support. He'd have a thing or two to say about that. Then the laughter faded. Marion Gunner's face eased into a swollen, self-serving, vacant stare.

"You know you're turning into one hell of a pushy woman," he said. "I hardly recognize you."

"We can go anywhere you like," she said. "It doesn't have to be fancy. I just want to get away for a while."

"I don't know if I like pushy women."

"Ah, c'mon Gunner. What do you want me to do?"

Gunner's stare became a smile.

"Tell you what, Suzanne. You go back upstairs and put on that slinky blue silk thing you used to wear. I'll wait right here in the car."

"But Gunner. I can't wear that one anymore. The way it rides up my hip and grabs me all the way around, why I feel . . . I feel absolutely naked."

"That's the one, Suzanne. I'll be waiting right here."

Gunner looked his wife over to the stairs, and then his white crescent moon of a smile widened. Suzanne blinked and looked away. *That one there he's a devil he is I told her so but she didn't listen aint no other kind show off his own wife like that good Lord why she might as well be naked for the whole world to see why he oughtta be ashamed of himself there's some things a man just don't do he oughtta have his little pecker chopped clean off that'd teach him teach him good.* That's what her mother would've said. She had warned Suzanne not to run off with Gunner. But Suzanne was also excited by her young husband's sudden phosphorescent fervor, for it had been several months, possibly a year, since she had aroused in him even the mildest form of predatory interest.

Less agitated now, and in fact somewhat confident, she retraced her path around the car to the stairs and moments later her shadow flitted in through the door of the garage apartment. She did not bother about Robey or his wife, who both stared at her mutely but alertly from the darkened kitchenette like two animals trapped in a culvert, for she had nothing yet to tell them. She stepped past the three runty, red-haired boys, who were sleeping in spite of they smelled a little like mules, for they hadn't bathed in over a week, and how noisy they were, she thought, the way they snored and grumbled and cried out, it was a wonder she and Marion hadn't heard them before from the car, above even the sounds of the bottles and their parent's husky laughter, the boys clumped together on a stained, weather-worn mattress which she had found out back among the weeds and the broken glass and some empty *Sears Weatherbeater* paint cans and a few rusted pieces of iron, and which her brother had carried up and laid in the hall between the bedroom and the bath. In a hurry of unashamed expectation, she wiggled herself into the dress, and then, still wiggling, down the unpainted stairs and into the car.

"That's the one, Suzanne. It looks good. That's the goddamn dress I was talking about."

The boisterous, boyish-faced Marion Gunner then jerk-started the car, and a heavy cannonade of blueish smoke spilled out of the exhaust pipe. Then the rusted blue Pontiac skidded back out of the drive, lurched one way then another, and sped off into the swarmy dark.

The rusting hulk of a trailer set back in a stand of pines. A corrugated, green plastic awning fixed to one side, a makeshift porch complete with hanging plants and empty beer cans and a few mismatched pairs of boots. Among the litter of the sandy, weedy yard was everything from bottle caps and tiny, plastic shovels to abandoned radio parts and rusted tools. Also the skeletal remains of several ancient bicycles. And off to one side there was a blue '37 Packard, stolen or borrowed long ago but now forgotten in the smouldering shadows of the pines like the denuded carcass of some prehistoric behemoth left to rot. The doors were missing. The windows broken. Bits of glass were scattered randomly across the sun-speckled dash, across the floor. Three or four rheumy-eyed dogs slumbered noisily underneath. And out front there were a couple of tractor tires filled with dirt, which had once been planted with dahlias or begonias or maybe black-eyed Susans, but were now sandboxes for an unwashed, fidgety, red-haired brood of slue-footed and seemingly genderless children with their gaping, choking, almost unintelligible cries of sibling rivalry.

Then came the shrill, fluting voice of their mother from the back of the trailer. "You go on leave your sisters alone Robey. They aint doing you nothing. You hear me Robey? If I catch you at it again I'm gone beat the fire out of you."

The children scattered.

The place they were going to was a roadside bar about a mile from the Jacksonville Naval Air Station called The Hanger, which was the first time for Suzanne, but Marion, since he worked at the NAS as a navy cook, had stopped there on more than one occasion, it being directly on his way home. The Hanger wasn't really a hanger. It was more like an abandoned chicken shed, complete with corrugated tin roof, that had somehow escaped becoming a strip mall. But in a spirited effort to attract navy fliers and flight mechanics, the owners had hung a few plastic model planes from the ceiling and slapped a few black and white photographs on the wall. Charles Lindbergh after he had landed in Paris. Amelia Earhart before she was lost. One from 1944 of a couple of Hellcats on top of a sun-gleaming aircraft carrier somewhere in the Pacific. And there were many more photos besides with smiling, bright-toothed pilots giving the thumbs-up sign. (Suzanne, when she saw them, thought the pilots all looked like Clark Gable, and said so, but Marion didn't hear her.) The waitresses all wore leather jackets, aviator glasses, mini skirts, and cowboy boots, all in keeping with the earnestly pro-aviator atmosphere. They served a dark beer they called The Red Baron, and whiskey in mugs. But in spite of all this, the plastic models and the photographs and the waitresses in their aviator costumes, the clientele was decidedly non-Navy, except for Marion Gunner. Outside there was a bright yellow neon sign which hummed noisily, and blinked a steady, happy, mindless, "YES WE'RE OPEN."

As they neared this chicken shed of a bar, Marion nudged his wife and grunted something she could not make out, and then they skidded into the unpaved strip of parking lot, which was already full of Pontiacs and Firebirds and dusty, flatbed pick-ups. Marion pulled around to the back and parked near an industrial garbage bin caught in the haze of a dim-glowing security light. He jerked the keys from the slot. Then he and his wife of the slinky, blue dress got out and walked inside.

"Hey there Gunner. Where you been?"

"The hell with Gunner. Would you look at what's with him!"

"That's just what I'm doing. Goddamn. Gunner, boy, aint no doubt about it. Looks like you've been holding out on us. Pull up a chair. Pull up two."

The voices belonged to a group of men sitting around an unwashed, black-topped Formica table near the front, near a window, the yellow of the neon sign outside flashing rhythmically, happily across their drunken soiree, three heads arched back in dilatory repose and then lurching forward with concupiscent grins. Above them the air was stagnant and hot with the smoke of several packs of Camels.

"You aint never brought nothing like her before."

"Darling, whatch you doing with Gunner here?"

"What's your name?"

"Boys," said Marion, "this here's Suzanne. Suzanne, that's Mike, the one slobbering over his beer. That one there is Pete. Looks like he's slobbering over you. And the one with the Camel's growing out of his ears, that's Danny Boy."

"Good evening there, Suzanne," said the slobbering Pete. His close-cropped hair and his overweening, red-faced, lurching leer gave the distinct appearance of inbred idiocy. He peered through a couple of empty beer bottles as he spoke. "You're just about the prettiest little thing I've ever seen. I hope you don't mind. I just wanted you to know."

"Good evening yourself," said Suzanne, but she tossed him a smile anyway, and then one to the others, Mike and Danny Boy, who had nothing more to say, it seemed, their bloated faces now blinking happily in the wash of the yellow neon light from outside, and then she slid some closer to Marion and squeezed hold of his arm. In the stupefying, hazy, beer-smelling excitement of the bar she had seemingly forgotten about her brother and his family hiding out in the garage apartment. But then she and Marion had only just arrived. He was not yet ready for the news. She squeezed his arm with greater force, almost fiercely. If she had had the strength she might have twisted it off. Then Marion waved over one of the aviator waitresses with his free hand and ordered a couple of Red Barons. His three buddies ordered the same.

"So, Gunner," said Danny Boy, "what's the word? We aint seen you in so long we started to feel left out. Thought maybe you had forgotten about us little people. What's the word, boy? What's the goddamn scuttlebutt out of the Pentagon."

"Yeah, Gunner," said Pete. "What are they going to do about them hostages they snatched up in Liberia?"

"That's Libya, you fool," said Mike.

"Well where ever the goddamn hell it is. What are they gonna do?"

"I'll tell you what I'd do," said Danny Boy. "I'd send in old Gunner here with a pocket full of dynamite and a Swiss Army knife. Talk about your Ollie Norths. Them sorry hostages wouldn't stand a chance."

"Them terrorists, you mean," said Mike.

"Yeah, that's what I meant. The bastards."

For a time the talk drifted about the table like the smoke from the Camels, moving from the plight of potential hostages to Marion's supposed expertise in covert operations, which Danny Boy said he must have learned in the jungles of Central America, to the pasty, web-footed bastards in Congress who had probably caused the whole mess anyway. They all agreed they'd vote Republican the next time or die trying. The beers came and went. More beers were ordered. Then a couple of aviator mugs of whiskey. A burst of raucous, degenerate laughter. And it soon became clear to Suzanne that Marion's inveterate bar buddies, not having anything remotely to do with the military themselves, thought him a decorated veteran of two or three wars, and an advisor to the generals of several failed coups. At least that's the impression they gave.

Then Suzanne began thinking about how and when she would tell her husband about her stepbrother, Robey, and his wife waiting in the kitchenette, and also the three, small boys sleeping in the hall. Marion was surely drunk enough, the way he now kept his head turned slightly to one side, the way he spoke in halting, ominous pronouncements. But Suzanne was unsure how to break through this blurring rain of masculine exaggeration. What would she say? She was also afraid of how Marion would react. *Gunner? What? It's about my brother, my stepbrother I mean, you see he's down on his luck and needs a place to stay for the night, or maybe longer. What fucking stepbrother? And there's his family, too. I said what fucking stepbrother? Well I guess it just never came up before, but he's down on his luck just now and he – Goddamn fucking parasites. This aint no goddamn hotel. I know Gunner. I know. You tell your goddamn stepbrother that. I'm sorry. I'll tell him. Sorry my ass.* So in her palsied, somewhat drunken state of mind, she said nothing, she'd wait, at least for the moment, and instead, she listened to the smokey blur of masculine voices, the words fading in and out, blinking, blinking, like the happy, yellow neon light outside, and her own thoughts fading in and out as well in stark counterpoint.

" . . . and that's when that goddamn F-14 turned its nose straight down and buried itself in the goddamn jungle. Biggest fucking fireball you ever saw. And the Colombians, hell, they didn't even look for survivors. They just walked."

"Damn, that's cold."

"That's Colombians for you. Biggest pricks there is."

The air was quiet around the trailer, hot, and it *smelled of tar and turpentine, and ever so faintly, the brackish, salty, oily smell of the bay. They had pulled the front seat out of the '37 Packard and flopped it up against the trailer under the corrugated, green plastic awning, which is where the oldest girl and her mother now sat. The strange, silent stepbrother was gone now. He had a wife and children of his own. And the two sisters and the dogs were off somewhere in the woods. But the father was there, rummaging through a sink full of dirty dishes, maybe a week's worth, looking for a suitable coffee cup. He was cursing and apologizing by turns. It was Sunday.*

"And I suppose you'll be telling me next you love this boy."

"He's not a boy, Mama."

"Well he's sure not much of a man. I'm telling you Love's Baby in my day, and that wasn't too long ago, a man made himself known. If he loved a young girl, and I mean if he wanted to marry her outright, there was plenty of that other stuff going on, but that aint what I mean, why the first thing he'd do he'd sit up with her folks, sometimes the whole night. That's what he'd do. That was a young man making himself known. What he intended to do. Why Love's Baby, sweetheart, we don't know anything at all about this boy of yours. He aint come by even once."

"Mama, he didn't come by 'cause he didn't know where to go."

"He probably just some red-headed peckerwood wanna stick his whole self in a hole."

"Mama!"

"I'm sorry Love's Baby, but there's a lot in this world you just too young to know about. Your Daddy, now he did right by me, and him already with a boy of his own. That's why I'm always gone to think of you as Love's Baby. But there's more than you can shake a stick at would've hitched up their pants and been gone the next morning without so much as a peep good-bye. That's the way a lot of them

were. Still are. I know exactly what I'm talking about, sweetheart."

"But Mama, he aint like that. He's a Navy man. I met him three months ago and we've been going out every Saturday night since. He's been transferred to Jacksonville. He's going today, and I'm going with him."

"Love's Baby, sweetheart, I just don't like it. If you've been gone with this boy for three months, why aint he been out to see us? Some no-account. He's up to something, that's for sure. I can feel it."

"Mama, I already said. I didn't tell him where to go."

"You what?"

"I didn't tell him."

The mother now staring at the daughter, lips pursed, face pinched and red, and the daughter looking at nothing in particular, maybe the greenish light filtering through the green plastic awning and dancing on the ground.

"Love's Baby, I'll say it now. You've got some furious gall about you. You ashamed of your family? You ashamed of where we live? Let me tell you your Daddy been scratching out some way to live since before you were born and he aint never asked nothing from no man. There aint many men like that. He deserves better. And so do I."

"I'm sorry, Mama."

"Sorry don't do it, Love's Baby. You want to go dancing around with this navy boy, well you go right ahead. But don't you sorry me. Why, if you weren't so big I'd give you a whipping myself. Lord knows it'd be the right thing to do."

"Mama, I'm sorry."

Then there was silence. It was cooler sitting under the green awning, but not much. The daughter went into the trailer. A few strange, inarticulate sounds from the father, the daughter saying yes daddy, no daddy, yes daddy, and then she returned to the musty, lump of a '37 Packard front seat, a small, flowery suitcase in her hand. She wore a look of desperate apology. Her mother did not look up.

"Mama, I'm going now. I'm catching a Greyhound out of Milton at 1:00. I'll tell him, Mama. I'll tell him about you and Daddy. But not just now. After we get married. Then I'll tell him. Bye Mama. Don't you worry now. Good-bye."

And then she was gone. The sunlight still filtered green through the green awning, and everywhere the heat swarmed. Looking up, the mother squinted in the direction of the road, but she couldn't see past the splintered mailbox. The father looked out from the doorway.

"She's gone now, Daddy. Our little Love's Baby is gone away."

"I can see that, Merle."

"But she oughtn't of done it like that. Just up and gone. She should've told somebody what she had in mind."

"Hell, Merle, that's what she was trying to do."

The yellow neon sign outside was still blinking with happy regularity, but inside a change had come over the bar. The smoke seemed thicker now, and the once contemporary track lighting less bright, which suggested, at least to Suzanne, the huddling, hushed atmosphere of a cave. The men sitting around her, still talking in their exaggerated and pointlessly random way, they became almost primeval in this vision of her detachment, the stale-beer smell, the heavy, musty, sweat-smell, the unnoticed litter of cigarette packages, tiny Camels crumpled up, scattered across the table. She looked at their meaty, sloping shoulders, their too dark eyes lost in the even darker shadows of their brows, their faces ripe with the memory of anthropoidal belligerence. She shuddered slightly, instinctively, then gulped down the last of the Red Baron in front of her and began to feel better. She had all but forgotten the problem of her brother.

" . . . It's like I was saying," said Marion, drinking as he spoke. "They should have blown that fucking Ayatollah away soon as they saw there was trouble. That was back in '72 and they just stuck their heads in the sand. There's been hell to pay with them ragheads ever since."

"I was against him the first time I heard about him," said Pete. "Ayatollah. What kind of a name is that?"

"That aint his name," said Danny Boy.

(Mike laughing into a mug of whiskey.)

"Well what is it then?" said Pete.

"He's like a pastor. Sort of. That's what they call 'em there."

"Hell, that's even worse."

Then the conversation faded. The waitress came with some more beer and this time Pete paid and they began to drink. From the juke box near the back of the bar there was a twangy Willie Nelson song, and in the reddish glare of that juke box there was a couple dancing, though there wasn't really a dance floor, they had just pushed back some of the tables and started whirling on the scuff marks. Then Danny Boy said how he hadn't done any dancing in a long while, and Mike and Pete both nodded, and then all three looked at Suzanne and said why not, even if it was the less than melodious Willie Nelson. Suzanne just blinked, but Marion said he didn't mind and told her to go to it, he wasn't much for dancing anyway, he was three left feet, and then he laughed. Before Suzanne could say a word against it, Danny Boy was dragging her towards the scuff-marked floor and the reddish, twangy-voiced, juke box glare of Willie Nelson (a second song), which in Suzanne's muffled, bewildered state reminded her of a pig roasting slowly on a spit.

They didn't dance long. Danny Boy, it seemed, had four left feet, and he kept trying to prop himself up by resting his head on Suzanne's shoulder and his hands firmly on her rounded, slinky, blue dressy behind, but she kept shaking herself free. Then Pete and Mike said it was their turn and they shoved Danny Boy into the juke box, but they couldn't decide who should go first, so they just stood there dumbly in the glare of the music (still Willie), each holding on to one of Suzanne's arms, and then Danny Boy came stumbling back from the juke box, for he felt he had hardly been given a fair chance, but he fell nearly on top of the now stationary Suzanne, his hands grabbing once again at her dress, him sliding down to the floor and the dress tearing slightly, and his head coming to rest between her ankles. Of course in the wake of this sudden and unexpected onslaught, Suzanne screamed, instinctively, though not violently, it was more of a choked-off, coarse kind of scream, but then she was trembling, slightly, and she probably would have collapsed altogether had it not been for the inadvertent support of the befuddled and now thoroughly alarmed Mike and Pete. It was then that Marion appeared. He had been dozing slightly at the table when his wife screamed, had then scattered a few empties with a sudden, jerking sweep of his arm, and the next thing he knew he was hurling himself towards the makeshift dance floor. Without wasting a motion, he wrenched free his wife.

"What in the hell you all think you're doing?" said Marion. "My wife she wanted to dance. That's dance you bastards. One at a fucking time. Not some goddamn fucking orgy."

And then Danny Boy, getting to his feet.

"Now hold on Gunner. There was just some confusion here about who was next. Aint that so, boys?"

Pete and Mike murmuring in perturbed agreement.

"Hell, Gunner boy, we didn't even know she was your wife. She sure is a good looker."

Pete and Mike murmuring some more.

"We didn't mean nothing by it, Gunner. Just having a little fun. That's all."

But Marion didn't hear him. He and his wife of the slinky, blue though slightly torn dress had already left the glare of the juke box and the twangy voice of Willie Nelson still singing in the background. Then they were gone from the bar altogether.

"He's a bastard. That's what he is," said Mike.

"Shut up," said Danny Boy.

For maybe twenty minutes nobody spoke. Robey and his wife sat rigidly, silently on the lumpy beige sofa in the front room, their heads turned towards the row of front room windows overlooking the drive below and the street beyond. They stared intently at the bright, naked, sweltering heat of the afternoon washing across the grassy yard next door and Mr. Guernsey's bungalow and Mr. Guernsey himself out there working on his azaleas. Their three runty boys were also quiet, sitting in a tangled clump some few feet from the sofa, on the edge of the rug, pasted over with sweat, exhausted, with runty quiet looks cast up towards their father, their mother, mostly their mother. Suzanne brought out some sandwiches and pickles and a couple of bags of pretzels and put them on the water-stained, mahogany table. There were Cokes for the boys. The adults drank from Marion's cache of beer.

"I thank you for taking us in like this Suzanne," said the brother. "We've had one God-awful time of it the last few days. Well, it's been longer than that if you ask Lillian here. But it's the last few days on the road that's been the worst as far as I'm concerned. I didn't think we'd make it."

"But what happened, Robey? What are you doing here?"

"He lost his job," said Lillian. "That's what he's doing here. Though why he went and picked this place I don't know. We could have gone to Mobile. I told him so. I have a brother there would have been no problem for him."

"That's enough, Lillian."

"That is not enough. You look around you. Why they aint much better off than we are. What do you expect them to do? I'm only thinking of the boys, Robey. I'm --"

"I said that's enough, Lillian."

The wife closed her mouth and slouched back on the sofa, her partially eaten meal of sandwich and pickle on a plate in her lap. The brother finished off one pickle and began on another, while the sister went into the kitchenette for some more beer. The sister returned. Then the wife called out to the boys, who, being done ahead of the adults, had turned the rug on the floor into a stormy, battle-plagued sea and their empty-though-crumb- covered plates into islands and their Coke cans into battle ships. "You boys you all get a move on now, you hear me, if you want to roughhouse like that then you better get your skinny little behinds outside before I swat you one." Then she got up herself, a bit flushed in the face from yelling at her grimy and suddenly bewildered progeny, marshalled them into the alcove kitchenette with their empty plates and their empty cans, and then hustled them outside and down the stairs. Silence. The brother finished the last of the pickles, slowly, and when the wife did not return, he relaxed. So did the sister.

"She's a hard woman. But she's a good woman."

"You're lucky, then."

"I know it. I know it. And that's making things all the worse. I mean here I've been working in that Navy Store going on ten years now and they lay me off just like that. I didn't tell her for a week. And then we figured to make a start of things somewhere else and I said here. And if not here maybe we'll head north to Georgie. Even further if we have to. I aint asking for handouts, Suzanne. I just figured you could put us up for a while give me a chance to look around. I could maybe find something. I know I could."

"I don't mind it, Robey. But I have to ask Marion first."

"Your husband? He wouldn't take too kindly having strangers move in. Hell, Suzanne, I don't blame him. It's a damn nuisance. And it aint like we've ever been real close neither. It's just, well, I thought --"

"It's not that, Robey. I just need to talk to him. That's all. He don't like surprises. But he's a good man down deep. I know he's a good man. I'll just break it to him easy. You know, maybe him and me go out drinking maybe some dancing and then when he's in a good mood I'll tell him. Now I can't promise you for sure, but I think he'll say yes to a couple of days."

"That's all I was thinking, Suzanne. Thank you."

By the time Marion and Suzanne skidded into the driveway, it was something past two in the morning. All the way home Marion had been making like a fighter pilot with the wheel, his rusted blue Pontiac lurching first one way and then another, riding up on the sidewalk, rattling off against a few garbage cans, plowing over a few fence-posted mail boxes, and all the while he was cursing the Ayatollah and them goddamn ragtag ragheads. Suzanne had been laughing, though she herself could not have said why, and she was still laughing when they pulled into the drive. Immediately the car stopped and a puff of blueish smoke coughed itself up from the exhaust pipe and then dissipated, and then Marion got out. Suzanne could see the thin, white-shirted, wavering line of an arm and shoulder as he rounded the car, then the halting jerk of his head as he bent to her window and said "C'mon Suzanne. Let's get you out of that goddamn fucking dress." The swarmy dark obscured his smile. And hers. But in the lilt of that moment she remembered about her brother and Lillian sitting in the dark of the kitchenette and the three runty boys asleep on the mattress, and why hadn't she told Marion earlier, she'd watched him drink at least seventeen beers, or maybe that was all of them did that, Danny Boy and the rest, she wasn't sure, but then he'd said he didn't want to dance and Willie Nelson blaring away and her dress getting torn and someone had screamed and she had just forgotten, that's all, maybe she could get him upstairs quick, past her brother and the rest before he saw, and he'd fuck her, a furious fuck, that's what he wanted, and then he'd fall hard asleep and she'd tell him in the morning, that was it, that was the time, but she'd have to stay close to him now. But Marion jerked his head back, and before Suzanne could say a word, he was up the stairs, and then his white-shirted arm and shoulder passed through the slit of the blackened screen door.

For a moment nothing happened, and Suzanne wondered if perhaps her brother and his family had left. But she remained in the car, in the catatonic refuge of her confusion. Then someone flicked on the kitchenette light, a hazy glow spreading out towards the front room, the screen covered windows, and Marion's voice came booming out through the haze. "Just who the fuck are you people?" And then a sharp, small voice. The wife. Lillian. "Are you going to let him talk to us like that, Robey? What kind of a man are you?" And then the husky, fatigued voice of the brother, only Suzanne could not make out the words, and then Marion booming some more and the wife making little sharp, clicking sounds and then the brother again. Then the kitchenette light was flicked off and there was a moment of penetrating silence. A dish or a couple of dishes or maybe the whole rack fell to the floor. Lillian's voice rose in sharp but pleading fury, but then became strangely inarticulate, almost strangled, and was followed by the strained, muffled groans of either Marion or Robey, or maybe both, Suzanne could not tell, and also short bursts of impotent rage. Then there were ominous thudding sounds vibrating straight through the garage apartment floor down to the driveway below, as if someone were turning over the front room furniture, heaving chairs about, then heading into the bedroom and attacking the bureau, the night table, then back into the front room. A lamp broke through one of the dark screens and fractured itself on the drive. The voices of the three runty boys, now awake, followed the lamp, come on daddy, get him, get him, pound that bastard, come on daddy, come on. Then the screen door banged open and shut and there was Lillian toe-footing it down the stairs, and she stopped at the car.

"Suzanne, they'll kill each other. What are we gonna do? You aint got a phone up there, have you? I didn't think so. You know anybody close? We got to get some help. There's no stopping them just you and me."

Then the screen door banged open a second time, and then off its hinges and over the rail, landing in the weedy grass down along the side yard, chain-link fence, and out bounced the two feverishly engaged husbands in a kind of pugilistic symbiosis, though it was quite clear this joining was the result of too little experience rather than too much (even in Marion's case), for they did not pummel each other so much as wrap their weak, wiry legs around weak, wiry legs (both men were the same height and weight, maybe 5'7" and 140 lbs.) and grab hold of each other's shirts and pull near, synchronously, in an effort to avoid blows by desperate, intimate proximity. They were like a single, struggling, gyrating insect in the fever of their rage, and in this way they bounced out of the apartment and down the stairs, and they flattened themselves against the rusted blue Pontiac.

Of course by this point the wives had fled in search of a telephone, but only just, and they turned when they heard the hollow thump on the car and looked back almost dolefully, and also hopefully, but then the men clambered to their feet and howled some at each other, insulted, angry, defiant, but wary, and then they resumed their dispute, so the two women left the driveway and cut across the sharp-bladed wet wet grass and past Mr. Guernsey's azaleas and then around to his front porch. Even as they pounded on the hooked screen door the howling and cursing and slobbering from the driveway sharpened, and the women had the odd sensation that their hair was falling out, so in a fit of despondency over both their husbands and their thinning hair, the women began shouting as well. Then there was a resounding click, and the bright yellow naked bulb of the porch light blinked on, and then the inner door seemed to fall away into the dark viscera of the house, and there, through the latticed obscurity of the black, black screen, they saw Mr. Guernsey's eighty-year-old face baffled by the heavy, wet, too-hot night and the madness in the driveway, and also by this sudden, insistent, womanly intrusion.

"What's all the to-do? What do you want? I'm warning you, I've got a dog in here?"

"It's all right, Mr. Guernsey. Please! Will you let us in?"

"Who are you?"

"I live next door, Mr. Guernsey. In the garage apartment."

"Then you better get back there, missy. They's two fellows right now looks like someone's gonna get theyselves killed for sure. They just this minute went around back of your place. They's mad as hell. I been watching from the window."

"Please, Mr. Guernsey. I need to get to a phone!"

And before he could question them further, they squeezed past him and came to a small telephone on a table in the narrow, dark hall. (Mr. Guernsey following them.) "You've been here before, aint you," he said. "I knew I'd seen you. Well, be quick about it. I aint used to staying up all night."

But Suzanne was already dialing, and then speaking in a quick, hushed, deliberate voice into the receiver, the stream of her words a garbled, almost inaudible mass of pure emotion as far as the grim and bitter Lillian could tell. Then Suzanne hung up the phone and the two women hurried into a small, dark sitting room off the even darker hallway, where the elderly and all too easily distracted Mr. Guernsey now stood in front of a large, uncurtained plate-glass window watching the slapstick proceedings of the driveway. It was like watching an old movie on the big screen. Both husbands had returned from their hasty, more-punches-thrown-than-landed sojourn in back of the garage apartment, and had brought with them several of the empty *Sears Weatherbeater* paint cans found there in the weedy grass, though the cans were apparently not so empty, for the two born-again vaudevillians were covered with splotches of paint, as was the driveway itself, and there was even some on the rusted blue Pontiac. The men were now busy hurling the empties back and forth over the top of the car, in this battle of their unbending wills, and cursing heavily with the effort, and ducking whenever a can came too close. Suzanne leaned up against a set of Wernicke brand glass-door bookcases and watched Mr. Guernsey watching. Her now somewhat overwhelmed sister-in-law sat in a faded Victorian-style chair and watched the wall instead.

Then Mr. Guernsey spoke up.

"This sure is one hell of fight there, missy. Would you look at them boys go at it. But them little kids up there, now, they just gonna get in the way."

And with that the wife of the grim and bitter repose looked up from her faded Victorian-style chair, and the sister also, with an expression now of befuddled fatigue suffusing her face, and there on top of the unpainted stairs sat the three runty boys, a bag of pretzels between them, the boys digging into the bag and stuffing their mouths and then hooting some at Marion and urging their pale and overwrought father to pound the bastard some more and give him some of this and some of that, and then one of the boys took aim with a fully rounded pretzel and let it fly in the general direction of the two combatants below, and then the others did the same, and then the bag was empty and there were pretzels scattered all over the paint-streaked driveway. Then the boys took up their hooting once again, but in the oblivion of their exuberance, they failed to see their mother and their aunt rounding the corner of the neighbor's house, grim, intent, but overly tired faces, for the two women had immediately vacated the dark confines of Mr. Guernsey's study upon seeing the boys, they would have nothing more to do with their husbands, let the police take care of them, and serve them right, all this foolishness keeping everyone up half the night, and waking the children, too, the two women then passing in front of Mr. Guernsey's movie-screen view, and him cursing some under his breath and hollering for them to get out of his way, for the battle looked to be reaching a climax, but the women were already marching up the stairs, driving the three runty, squealing boys like pigs into the darkened clutter of the garage apartment. Then they locked the door.

As for the husbands, they had soon tired of hurling cans, and in the sudden distraction of their wives going up the stairs, one of them, it was difficult to say which one because of the dark and the paint, broke away from the car and headed down the driveway, and he was just about even with the back of Mr. Guernsey's front porch when the second one tackled him from behind. In this the dream of their exhaustion the two men rolled off the cement pavement and across the wet wet grass and then into the shadow of a couple of azaleas up close to the house, which meant that Mr. Guernsey could no longer see them from his movie-screen window, so he cursed some more and trundled from the dark study into the even darker hall and then into the front corner bedroom and another, smaller window, him catching a sudden glimpse of someone's shoulders pulling up and away, and then some more shoulders, and a paint-covered back, and then everything fell back down to the grass again, and Mr. Guernsey realized the two men were struggling a little too near his azaleas. He opened the window and yelled down through the screen for them to watch out they better move their wrestling out a bit into the grass where he could see them better, but they went into the azaleas anyway, and then a few moments passed and they were out and around to the front of the house and down to the flagstone sidewalk, one shouting you bastard, you goddamn bastard, and the other shouting bastard back, and Mr. Guernsey now trundling from his corner bedroom down the hall and around to the still open front door, him thinking first of the word bastard, and reveling in its having been spoken, and then of his azaleas and were they all right and what the hell were those boys doing he better have another word with them, and then he looked out through the mesh of the front door screen, and he was just about to give them a piece of his mind when, suddenly, the two unreasoning and volatile husbands clambered up onto his porch, their shirts soaked with paint and sweat and streaked with grass stains and dust, and in a rush of fatigued inspiration they grabbed for one of the two large pink cement flower pots placed directly on either side of the crumbling front steps. They both picked the same pot, which may have been just as well, for in their weakened condition neither could have lifted a single flower pot unaided, but just what they intended to do with the one now firmly in both pairs of hands was impossible to say. The two men staggered towards the center of the porch and stopped beneath the hot burning naked bulb of the porch light, the pot listing dangerously to one side. A look of frustrated, murderous, even painful rage came to both faces.

"Bastard," said the one.

"Bastard," said the other.

And then, with a surprisingly vigorous and also simultaneous heave, the men yanked at the doubly-clutched pot, and in so doing they yanked themselves free and fell backwards onto the grimy porch floor, and the pot, for a moment it hung there in the yellowish, burning, even feverish light, as if from a tether, and even Mr. Guernsey wondered what kept it up, but then it crashed in a heap of cement shards and cakes of dry, gritty dirt. There were no flowers, for Mr. Guernsey had planted none in over twenty-two years.

It was at this moment that the police arrived in two burnished squad cars. The two husbands did nothing. They seemed incapable even of thought and sat in a sort of stunned and exhausted silence, subdued, their shirts now covered with the dry flower pot dirt as well as the paint, as if the wild mania of before had evaporated into the swarmy, steamy dark. Then Mr. Guernsey burst through the screen door and across the porch and hailed the squad cars in his harsh voice of an old rooster. Two officers got out, one with a metal-backed notebook in hand, which he immediately flipped open and began writing in, and the other with a hand firmly planted on his holstered gun. The two met Mr. Guernsey in the middle of the once elegantly kept flagstone sidewalk.

"It's about time you all got here," said Mr. Guernsey.

"Are you the one called for the 911?" said the second officer.

"I sure as hell did."

"What's your name, sir?" said the first officer.

"Guernsey. Walter Jacob Guernsey. What in the hell kept you boys?"

"We came as soon as we got the call, Mr. Guernsey. Now what seems to be the problem?" It was the first officer again, and he seemed to be writing down Mr. Guernsey's answers verbatim.

"It's them two right there," said Mr. Guernsey, waving his arm aggressively, eagerly perhaps, in the direction of the porch. "Yes sirree Bob. They were hooting and howling in fits all over the goddamn neighborhood and trying to bust into people's homes, and then they tried to get into mine, only they didn't, I told them I got a dog, shouted out to them from the porch was the way I done it, and I had a shovel in my hand too, but then they come back a while later and grabbed a hold of that flower pot and smashed it up just like it is now. They aint nothing but some crazy mad dogs got loose, the both of them, oughtta be locked up, now you write it down good, son, just like I'm telling you, I've a mind to press charges, you write that down too, that's a fact."

Both officers nodded, and Mr. Guernsey, feeling he had said all he had to say, went over to look at the squad cars. Then the one with the notebook flipped it shut and both he and his partner went up to the porch. Neither husband had moved since the flower pot had crashed. They sat in almost prayerful silence. But also a rigid, defiant, even contentious kind of silence, at least when it came to answering questions from the police. Or not answering them. So the officers had no choice, really, but to cuff the two brazenly inert husbands and lead them back to the squad cars and plop them inside, which they did, and then almost immediately both prisoners fell asleep.

And that was the end of it as far as the officers were concerned. But for Suzanne it was more of a beginning. She was looking down upon her husband and her stepbrother and the squad cars in the street. She was standing beside the lumpy, beige sofa, looking out from the row of front room windows, holding the chintz curtain a shadow to her face in case someone looked up her way. She asked herself why she hadn't told Gunner about her family years ago. The truth was she hadn't wanted him to know. The trailer of her growing up just rotting away there in the woods, and the suffocating closeness of six people in the clutter and stench of so small a space. She had felt contaminated by her family. That was why she'd run off with Gunner like she had. Like running away from the plague. But now, seeing her husband of five years up against Robey, she couldn't tell any difference between them. She'd been wrong to abandon her family like she did. She'd been wrong not to tell Gunner the first day she met him. And then suddenly she heard her mother's voice inside her head, or maybe it was her own voice colored now with a wisdom like her mother's. *You can't run away from yourself, Love's Baby, and until you realize that, aint nothing gonna work out the way you want it to.* She looked at her sister-in-law, Lillian, now asleep on the sofa. In the morning they would go down to the jail and get their husbands out. But not now. A night in jail would help to clear the air.

Then Suzanne let the curtain fall away from her face and moved away from the windows. The squad cars sped off, the red of their tail lights winking in the swarmy, heavy dark, and then they were gone altogether. And Mr. Guernsey, who had been admiring the sleek, burnished look of both cars, stared vacantly at the spot where they had been, and then he turned and went inside.

Blue Henry

It is the first week in August.   The air is hot with the dust of brick and tar and pine straw and grass. There has been no rain for days, weeks, though in the absence of reliable memory, the weeks might just as well be years.   And from out of this haze of heat and memory, a sandy-haired young man, everyone calls him Blue Henry, or just Blue, on account of the deep deep blue of his eyes, and a seriousness there which they mistake for sadness, he walks slowly, steadily, even purposefully down a dust-red road towards a small town, a sunken, washed-out kind of town, like footprints at the beach.   His only thoughts concern the buying and wearing of a suit, though they aren't his thoughts exactly, they come from Mr. Dobbs, from before, Blue stumbling out of his bunk in the early early morning then into the kitchen, firing up the stove, a pot of coffee working to a boil, then Mr. Dobbs coming in, sitting down, stiffly, the two of them talking, then not talking, then talking some more, then Mr. Dobbs working his own mouth to a boil, the red of his face about to bust from the pressure of a too-tight collar, the words then tumbling out like steam,

"What do you mean you don't have a suit? You been working my place close to five years now and you saying

you don't have a suit of your own? Christ Almighty, boy! Why you wouldn't have a pot to piss in if it weren't for me, now would you? Christ Almighty! You can't go to a funeral less you're wearing a good Sunday suit. You take this twenty dollars now and you go and buy yourself one. Don't take all day now. And don't go thinking this here's a gift, cause it aint. I'm taking it out of your wages. Now go on. Get moving."

So he had pocketed the twenty dollars, his features as calm and natural as unsifted earth in spite of the unexpected urgency of Mr. Dobbs' voice. It is only a suit for a funeral, after all, and for a man he never knew. He almost laughs at the thought. Then he crosses the old railroad tracks and turns down Dancy Street, past the red brick and the white awnings of the U.S. Post Office, past the unpainted clapboard austerity of Waldroop's Feed Mill, some men in short-sleeved shirts loading their wagons with cornmeal and flour and oats and lard, and when he nears the blackgreen porch of Laughlin's General Store, he stops. A couple of men in brown or beige hats are squatting down near the edge of the porch, a couple more are sitting on a hardwood bench set up against the wall, another is standing in the doorway, half-in, half-out, the screen door resting against his shoulder. The men seem content to pass the morning talking, older men they are, though not older than Mr. Dobbs, some chewing on dry stalks of grass, some not. They are talking about the murder of one Thomas Christian Cavanaugh, whose funeral is the reason Blue Henry needs a suit.

"Who do you s'pose done it?" says one with bigred ears and bald and his scalp patchy with sunburn. His name is Jake.

"Could've been anyone in this here town," says a second voice. "That's the way I see it. Why most anyone in this here town would of been proud to pull that trigger."

"Well it don't matter to me who done the shooting or why he done it," says the one in the doorway. "Done is done. That's what I always say."

The other men mumble in stubborn agreement, their pebbly-colored eyes narrowing fiercely, their collective pride hurt, it seems, because they had been left out of the shooting. Then a few words of inveterate speculation from one of the men on the bench, not the one with the bigred ears, this one is packing the bowl of a pipe with tobacco as he talks, the smell of stale smoke imbedded in his skin, an emptied pack of Granger Rough Cut in his shirt pocket.

"Well you'd have to say the fellow who done it had a pretty sharp eye whatever the reason. I've been down to where they pulled him out of the ditch and there wasn't any cover for had to been two hundred yards back on either side of the road. I figure whoever pulled the trigger he had to been waiting up in one of them live oaks on the Dobbs place. Had to had eyes like a goddamn panther too."

"Aint no one alive coulda done the kinda shooting you talking about, Earl," says Jake.

"Someone did it," says the second voice. The others nodding in unison, as if the unpretentious and somewhat vacantly expressed opinion that someone had done something was unequivocal proof of the doing. Then Earl continues.

"I figure how he had to been waiting up in them trees most of the day, and maybe he was getting stiff from sitting so long, and then again maybe he wasn't, but when he heard the steady hum of that black I-talian two-seater coming up the road, and when he saw how it was Mr. Thomas Christian Cavanaugh sitting sweet and pretty all by hisself, a goddamn clay pigeon sitting there, why he took up his Winchester, the kind with a silver breech, and whoever it was he just opened up and fired."

And with that the five men on the porch sink into a profound, if not astonished silence and contemplate the improbable death of Mr. Thomas Christian Cavanaugh. Blue Henry almost laughs at the mixture of awe and confusion spreading across their faces, but he too wonders who in the world could have shot at and killed someone from so a great distance, and at night too. Then he wonders how the five men could know all about the gun which had killed the unfortunate Mr. Cavanaugh and at the same time not know whose it was, how many Winchesters were there had a silver breech, and he is about to ask them outright when a black Model T truck with some pinewood side panels pulls up and the gravel crunching under the tires, but the driver he doesn't exactly get out, he cracks open the black door and stands up in the wedge of space between the door and the cab, him standing there on the greased side-step in a grease-stained fedora and waving at the men on the porch and his voice squawking away, say what you boys doing sitting there like lumps, hadn't you heard, there was some question about whether Mr. Cavanaugh was really dead or not, Farley Atkins said he saw him last night, he was coming home with his wife from her brother's house and the next thing he knew that blasted I-talian two-seater came blowing the dust off his front fender and there was Cavanaugh laughing like the devil to beat all, his wife didn't see it, she was asleep, but Farley swears by it, they all gathering down at Cooper's Funeral Parlor right now, they want to see the body but the Sheriff he aint letting them in, I don't know what's going to happen, but everybody's got a shotgun or a Winchester or something, I guess maybe they gonna see Cavanaugh in the ground one way or another. And with that the fellow in the truck slammed shut the door and his wheels spinning and the dust kicking up and off he went.

Cooper's Funeral Parlor was a one-story, brick building shaped like an el, and the bricks were painted a shiny, slick white. Out back there were dead azaleas up under the windows, and a hearse parked in the alley, and in the front there was a small, four-column porch and a scattering of white stone flower pots up around each column, though the pots were empty now except for the dust of a few unwatered chrysanthemums. There was also a narrow walk made from brick that wasn't painted white, the walk running from the steps to the street, the brick crumbling in places from the heat.

Half-a-dozen cars were parked along the curb and the Model T truck and a couple more cars had gone over onto the grass. A dozen rough-and-readies in work shirts and felt hats stood in front of the porch, their shirts stained with sweat and liquor and tobacco juice, the stains all up and down their backs and half-crescent moons under their arms, and them glaring at the white of the funeral parlor and the sun glinting off their shotguns. In the shade of the funeral parlor porch stood Sheriff D. W. Griggs, a skinny old bag of a man about sixty with a few strands of greasy white hair combed from one ear to the other and a few age spots or warts which had broken out on his neck, but with him in the shade and the others in the glare of the sun, it was impossible to see if he had a gun or not.

By the time Blue Henry and the five from Laughlin's made it over to the parlor, three of the rough-and-readies were engaged in a vigorous debate with the Sheriff, the rest watching and waiting from the safety of their indecision to see who was going to break first. The five from Laughlin's were holding shotguns like the rest, which they had borrowed from Laughlin himself, who was not present, but theirs were unloaded, for in their instinctive, desperate, almost manic hurry to reach the hub of so much civic controversy, they had forgotten about ammunition. But there they were just the same, sidling up to the clutch of waiting, nervous, expectant men and wondering how in the world someone could shoot at Mr. Cavanaugh and miss. Blue Henry was standing right alongside them, wondering pretty much the same thing, but without a shotgun.

"We gotta right, Sheriff, to see the body if we want to. How do we know he's really dead if we don't?"

"Take my word for it, boys," said the Sheriff. "He's as dead as they come."

"Now Sheriff, you know what Farley said."

"Farley was drunk," said the Sheriff.

"But what about our rights?"

"You all don't have any rights," said the Sheriff. "Not when it comes to eyeballing a deceased victim of an at-large criminal intelligence. You all know better than that."

"Come on, D. W. Just one look through the back door can't hurt nothing."

"Don't push it, boys. You all can see him when they lay him out. Just like anybody else."

"God damn it, D. W. How the hell long is that gonna be. They've been working on him for two full days now."

"You all just have to wait."

From the shade of the porch there was an ominous sounding click, and then silence, and Blue Henry thought it looked like the sheriff was grinning, but he couldn't tell for sure with the glare from the sun, and neither could the dozen rough-and-readies plus five, who as a group had more or less collapsed inward among themselves in a furry of impotent confusion. Then the one who had done most of the talking, an old fellow like the sheriff but with more hair, and a bulbous paunch that lapped over his belt, he began shouting and cursing and then he stepped towards the porch and raised his shotgun and two others filled in behind him and raised theirs as well, and Blue Henry couldn't tell exactly where they were aiming at, and most likely neither could they, because of the glare, maybe they figured D. W. Griggs had lived past his usefulness as Sheriff, or maybe they were aiming at the columns, or even one of the white stone flower pots. Nobody could tell. They raised their shotguns and began firing with simultaneous determination, but the first one, his gun jammed immediately, and the other two had forgotten about ammunition, the same as the five from Laughlin's porch, so all there was was a steady click, click, click, click, and then a couple of under-the-breath curses. Then the one with the jammed gun smacked it against the crumbling red brick walk and tossed it in the grass and left it there, and before anyone said a word he had driven off in a dull green Packard, the dust from his sudden departure settling unevenly on the windows of the other cars.

Of course that ended the stand-off at Cooper's Funeral Parlor. The rest of the men sunk into a profound, embarrassed silence, and then slunk off in two's and three's and the sound of car doors clacking shut and then motors puttering off into the steamy, hazy, smothering heat of a late August morning. And then Sheriff D. W. Griggs relaxed his grip on the shotgun he had been holding the whole time and headed from the white of the parlor and the shade of the porch to his own car parked in the grass, and he too drove away. Only Blue Henry remained, for he had brought with him no shotgun or Winchester and so felt no shame at being unable to get past a balding, age-spotted sheriff. He did not know how to feel. He had all but forgotten the need for a funeral suit and the twenty dollars in his pocket. Everything that had happened, from the men on the porch and their talk of shootings and murder and the mob and the squelched raid on the funeral parlor, he had witnessed with a thrilling, shuddering, incredulous excitement, for though he had never heard of such things happening in Pokalawaha, at least not that he could remember, he had always imagined them possible, and as he stood there now in the silence of the others having gone and the glare of the white building before him, all he could think about was Mr. Cavanaugh and how the man was surely dead, an incredible shot, certainly, the gunman hiding in the branches of one of the live oaks on the Dobbs place and then squeezing the trigger, but he was dead just the same, murdered.

Then Blue Henry closed his eyes, and he could actually see the thin, dark shadow of a Winchester stretching out before him, the sky becoming a deep, dark, blood-smeared red, and on the road he could see the unaware Mr. Cavanaugh grease-dusting the countryside in a black I-talian two-seater, a convertible, cloth covered seats, also black, the hum of the engine drifting up through the air, the smell of gasoline, of metal, then a crcrcrcraaaackckck, the body stiffening, lurching forward, the automobile lurching forward also, then the body tumbling to the bloodblackening ground, the body broken now, twisted, lying in the ditch, and the automobile also lying in the ditch, also twisted, the wheels spinning, spinning, the air growing heavy with darkness and smoke, and then the wheels not spinning. And this image became for Blue Henry a sort of memory, like pictures on a wall become memories, and so when Blue opened his eyes he wanted to chase down the men who had rushed Sheriff Griggs and tell them that Mr. Thomas Christian Cavanaugh was as dead as they come and he should know because it was he himself, Blue Henry, who had pulled the trigger.

It didn't matter that Blue had never actually been in the tree with a gun in his hand because Blue had a regular talent for re-creating the past. He could look at a picture of, say, a woman wearing a blue frock with a little bit of lace around the collar, the woman short, fortyish, a little bit plump, plump cheeks, plump lips, maybe even plump eyes, and he could think of her as his very own aunt if he felt the need of having one, call her Aunt Betty, and before too long that's who she'd be and then every time he'd look at her picture he'd remember himself as a little boy and her taking him on a picnic lunch somewhere along the Pokalawaha River, and maybe an ice cream afterwards. For the moment, then, Blue Henry had been the one to shoot Mr. Thomas Christian Cavanaugh while hiding in the darkness of a tree, though why he could not exactly say, the deceased now stretched out upon a table somewhere in the back of Cooper's Funeral Parlor, an absolutely round face, absolutely white eyes, black hair cropped close, though what Mr. Cavanaugh actually looked like, well Blue Henry couldn't say much about that either, and so it was only natural, wasn't it, that he wanted to fill in the gaps, to take a good look at the face of the man he thought he had killed,

at the face of death, so to speak, to know death by looking
at it, because death did not touch the young except
remotely, that's the way Blue felt about it, like reading in
the newspaper about earthquakes in Bolivia or a hurricane
in Texas or Louisiana, because there was no other way to
experience death and remain untouched. So Blue Henry
made his way to the back of Cooper's Funeral Parlor and
keeping as close to the white brick walls as he could, past
the el-shaped row of dead azaleas and the hearse parked in
the drive, and then he snuck inside.

For a long time he stood just inside the back screen door
and he did not move. He was standing there, looking down
a long, narrow hallway, a few doors open wide on both
sides, the light of several rooms slicing yellow and white
across the hallway floor. At the far end of the hall there
was a burgundy leather sofa with brass knobs nailed to the
frame, and a mahogany end table next to the sofa. Up on
the walls, neatly framed, there were pictures of coffins,
hundreds of carefully crafted coffins, walnut, maple, oak,
a few pine ones for the poor folks, and a few that looked
like they were made from brass with gold plated handles
attached for generals or admirals or maybe a few mayors.
But there were so many coffins that he really couldn't
distinguish one from another.

Then Blue Henry heard the voices.

"Just a little more wax oughta do it," said the first.

"If'n it don't get no hotter, you mean," said the second.
"Why you weren't finished with him but an hour this
morning when the wax it started beading up. Kind of like

he was sweating, I said to myself, and I admit I felt like pulling out my handkerchief and dabbing at his forehead, only I didn't, and then the next thing I know'd why them beads was rolling off of his cheeks and onto the table. Damnedest thing I ever saw. Looked like his whole face was melting."

The men stopped speaking for a moment, the hollow silence of exhausted concentration descending upon the white-brick building, upon the dead chrysanthemums and the crumbling walk, upon the one working wax into the face of a corpse, shoulders stooped and stiffening, the wax of life he'd said when the other had come to work for him, the gift of rosy-cheeked immortality, and the both of them had laughed at the thought; and the same hollow silence descending upon the other one, him standing a step or so behind and always so, a bleary and bespectacled eye peeping up and over the stooped and stiffening shoulder with a mortified and yet heartily insidious interest in the vanishing art of funeral preparation; and there was a silence about Blue Henry as well, though a different kind, him still standing in the hall, leaning back along the edge of the back screen door and the door giving a little because the hinges were loose, listening, inhaling slowly, holding his breath, wondering if he would recognize the face of the man he had shot at and killed, if anyone could recognize a face which had melted once and might do so again, the young man still holding his breath, then the voices of the two men once again, and the young man exhaling, slowly.

"This one's been too much work," said the first.

"Them was my exact words," said the second. "You s'pose he'll keep?"

"He'll have to," said the first. "I'm through with him."

"Dont blame you none at all," said the second. "You want we should dress him up now?"

The first shook his head, smiled, and then the two began to clean up. Then the first started talking about a Mr. Peterson who had passed on the week before last and how Mrs. Peterson had come in and slipped him a jug of something not too dry about an hour before they closed the lid. For the journey to the promised land she had said, and then the first he looked to the second and burst out laughing with that, and the second he was nodding slowly, thinking about the promised land, a bit bewildered, and then the first started in again about how he had figured the only place Mr. Peterson was going to was into the ground, at least for quite a while, and how he was a practical man so he had just waited till Mrs. Peterson went home and then he had slipped it from out of Mr. Peterson's bony white fingers, meaning the jug, and stashed it back of his mahogany desk. Then the first stopped talking and the two of them looked at each other, eye-to-eye twinkling, and then the first again.

"No sense letting it go to waste."

"Them was my exact words."

So the two men stepped into the yellow and white light of the hall, their voices burning with an up-till-then unconscious thirst, the first one wearing an ill-fitting white smock over a blue serge suit, not tall, not thin, bulbous rather, with black bulbous shoes rounding up from beneath the smock, rounding up and then down and then up and down the hardwood hall, the second one following close behind, smockless, serge-suitless, a pair of wire-rimmed spectacles dangling from a gold chain around his neck, the two men walking towards the burgundy leather sofa, the mahogany end table, then the hall jig-jagging left, the men turning past sofa and table, and all the while the various and vividly-imagined possibilities of Mr. Peterson's sprightly jug dangling before them, the first recounting with insouciant admiration a time not too long ago when the venerable and possibly alcoholic Mr. Peterson had passed up the pleasure of attending his own father's funeral in favor of standing outside the church, a double-barreled shotgun in hand, him calling out for some sign that God did or did not exist, some reassurance, perhaps, that death was not just a carnival sideshow, as he had put it, the dead nothing more than freaks to be caged and then put on display and then forgotten, and receiving no answer, at least at first, he had turned his gun in anger upon the bell-tower bell and began firing away, the rain of bird shot rising up and then down upon the hidden nests of blue-gray kites, him then laughing uproariously at the sight of all those birds whirling round and round the tower in a shit-ejecting panic, a sign it's a sign a sign, he had cried, the bird shit falling down upon his head with every shot then shout, him firing until he had exhausted his supply of cartridges then sinking to a squat amid the gelatinous offal of this blue-gray whirl, the birds unsettled still but empty as well, him still laughing; and the second one nodding politely at the first, wondering not about the filth of so many birds roosting in the tower and what had been done to clean them out, nor about the impact of Mr. Peterson's penny ante tirade on the general populace of Pokalawaha, the town not the river, and how ever since that theologically oriented shooting spree a man could get a week in jail just for pointing a gun at the church, no not about the stench of birds or the shooting at church bells, but about how many other jugs had been buried, the two of them unawares, and how could they get at them before the liquor turned sour and whose grave were they going to dig up first.

As soon as the two disappeared into Mr. Cooper's office, Blue slipped down the hall to the room where Mr. Thomas Christian Cavanaugh was. A naked body stretched out on a long, metal table, the body a flabby, grayish-white and a ragged patch job just above the ribs where the bullets had gone in. Behind the body there was a white marble-topped counter and a scattering of chrome silver instruments, some for prodding, for cutting, slicing, shaping, a few unlabeled bottles filled with red or purple or green liquid, a couple of syringes, and then Blue Henry surveying the entire room, a row of glass-windowed cabinets along the near wall, some more bottles, a few pans for drainage, some linens, a couple of wooden stools along the far wall and a couple of windows open above the stools and a hot breeze blowing in and the smell of dead azaleas and the dust-streaming sunlight. It was almost surreal the way death was all around and him looking at the corpse of Mr. Cavanaugh and this was his first corpse and then Blue Henry blinking with the realization that death was not so remote, which unhinged him a bit, so much so that right there he abandoned his claim to having shot the dead man, or perhaps it abandoned him, and he was just about to leave the funeral parlor altogether and go off in search of a fine serge suit to wear to the funeral when all of a sudden it seemed that he wasn't looking at a corpse, that the men had been right about Mr. Thomas Christian Cavanaugh not being dead, for there was the man himself, sitting on the end of the preparation table, giving Blue the once-over and sort of half-smiling, his legs dangling.

"So you were thinking I was dead, is that it son?"

Blue Henry said nothing. What could he say? Of course we thought you were dead, least that's what them down at Laughlin's were saying, aint you dead Mr. Cavanaugh, why there was that shot from up in one of them live oaks and what a shot it was why not one man in a million could of made that shot of course I didn't see it I wasn't even there I hope you didn't get the wrong impression I mean I wouldn't do something like that but did it hurt much I mean dying like that or maybe it happened so quick you didn't feel a thing is that what happened Mr. Cavanaugh, but Blue Henry didn't say a word, no, what could he say, why folks would think him crazy, even if they wouldn't say it, him standing there motionless, bewildered, could not could not could, could only continue his unblinking, throbbing, almost painful obeisance.

"I was the only one here when they laid me out, but that was a couple of days ago," the strangely undead Mr. Cavanaugh looking around the room, uncautiously, not so much to see what was there but to see what wasn't, and all the while talking on and on and on, "and don't you go thinking it was such a great shot neither, I know what they're saying and damn the lot of them for it, why nobody knows who killed me and nobody knows from where, not exactly, not even me," and then him noticing his burial clothes, a three-piece suit, gray, pin-striped, a red silk handkerchief stuffed into the front pocket of the jacket, the suit stretched out upon the counter top, and also a starched white shirt, stiff for the stiff, and a black, leather belt and a red silk tie, to match the handkerchief, but no shoes, and no socks, but hell, he wasn't going anywhere, and besides, who would look to see, and then Mr. Cavanaugh hopped down from the preparation table and headed for the suit and the rest and began to get dressed, "why the truth is probably nobody killed me, I probably killed myself, probably I just flipped that goddamn I-talian headache of mine and landed in a ditch, that's what it probably was, son, then maybe some son-of-a-bitch came along and saw me lying there dead and he pulled out a gun and plugged me with a couple just for good measure, that's what he probably did, most sons-of-bitches can't resist that kind of temptation, but what the hell, I can't say it bothered me any, I mean I was probably already dead," him buttoning the white shirt, adjusting the cuffs, pulling on the pants, the last of his flabby, grayish-white flesh being covered up and the place in his chest where the bullets went in, and still talking, talking, not so much to Blue Henry any more, or anyone, not even himself, he was just talking, and pretty soon Blue Henry was lost in the memory of those words, no longer the gunman, a spectator now, and whether it was truly his memory or not did not seem to matter, the car in the ditch and the wheels spinning and Mr. Dobbs marching out to see what happened, a Winchester in his hand in case it was trouble and a kerosene lantern because he couldn't see in the fading light, just a little bit of red along the horizon, what's going on out here what's that racket was anybody hurt or you boys just fooling around don't you all know this is private property can't you boys stay on the road, Mr. Dobbs not recognizing just yet, holding up a lantern so he could see, and then he saw, the light from the lantern glinting off the back fender, is that you Mr. Thomas C. Cavanaugh, what in the hell you doing boy, you better have this goddamn infernal I-talian car of yours removed come morning you goddamn bastard, you hear me boy, I'm talking to you, and then Mr. Dobbs not talking, noticing the dead Mr. Cavanaugh now for the first time and chewing some on his bottom lip and then setting the lantern on a smashed-up fender and poking at the body with his gun butt and the yellowish lantern light now splattering across his own face, which was void of any emotion, like the face of one dead man looking at that of another, and then in a single, sweeping, instinctive, motion he raised his Winchester and sent a couple of slugs into Mr. Cavanaugh's chest, the slugs coming out the other side and thudding into the ground. That's how it had happened, Blue Henry was sure of this now, it was Mr. Dobbs, it had to be, but before he could fully contemplate the whys and therefores of this murder of a dead man, he was startled from his thinking by someone shouting. "Hey! You there! Is that you Blue Henry? Say what the hell are you doing in there?"

Blue Henry turned towards the sound of the voice, but slowly, awkwardly, a look of bewildered innocence pasted across his face. Two red-faced men were standing in the doorway of the preparation room, one in a white smock, the other a step behind with a still bespectacled head peering up and barely over the shoulder of the first. Blue Henry was standing near one of the open windows, his back to the sun-dusty sunlight streaming in and past him, and the strangely undead Mr. Thomas Christian Cavanaugh was back on the metal preparation table, dead as they come, of course, Blue Henry realized that now, the wax used to bring life to his face once more beginning to melt. Then the voice of the one again, hey Blue, you hear, you hear what I said, what the hell, the two in the doorway stumpumping into the room, their blood thickening, quickening, one on either side of the metal preparation table, do you think you're doing in them clothes, them aint yours, and it was then that Blue looked down and saw that he was the one dressed in the three-piece suit, the white shirt, the red tie, the black belt, though how this had come about he could not exactly say, then the red-faced men rounding the table, the young man rolling up pants legs buttoning the vest, his own clothes in a pile on the floor, what in the world do you think you're doing Blue, him then scooping up his discards, stuffing them into the quite possibly jug-weary arms of the one or the other, then running past the now stationary and bewildered two but turning slightly as he ran, nodding, turning again, smiling, no sirs no sirs my mistake all mine, then turning a third time but bumping into the metal preparation table, catching his reflection in the metal and then moving past, and the corpse of Mr. Thomas Christian Cavanaugh sliding slowly up and over the edge then tumbling to the floor, never you mind sirs it was my mistake my mistake, the two now silent and watching helplessly from the corner of the room, the corpse coming to rest face down chin out on the cold cold tile, a small whitish pool of melting wax beginning to form beneath the lobe of one of the ears. But the young man named Blue Henry did not bother about the wax or the corpse or the two men watching, for he had his funeral suit now, and so he ran instead from the deepening silence of the preparation room into the late afternoon orange of the hall, and then out through the nearly unhinged screen door.

The Festival

$\mathbf{Me}$ and Ty we been sitting down on the stoop out front about an hour now, we waiting on Mama and Tramsee, and Im is wondering just where they at and what taking so long. Ty he saying say that how womens is, most likely they standing up front that old brass mirror hang on the wall in my mama keeping room and they primping with they hair the way they do it up and color they faces like they is thinking they still eighteen year old, only they aint, and Im is listening to Ty, only I really aint cause I looking up at the sky, and it almost dark and we go miss the parade they aint hurry up. Mama she and Tramsee been talking on that parade the whole while they been dressing theyself, and they voices floating out and down the porch like a shadow come before the rain.

"I aint live a day I be the one miss this parade," Mama say. "Why, we aint have one in eight or nine year now. You wunt here the last time."

"Well, I here now," Tramsee say, and sound like she smacking her lips together.

"It the cost of things what done most of them parades to death."

"Long as there a marching band, I aint mind the cost."

"You aint listening. You know how much it cost they hire out a marching band? Every dollar it worth you paying five."

"I heard a band one time up in Charleston. They was blowing they horns and dancing em up in the air and then down, and then they gone down the street, wunt nothing left but the drums. I'd a paid five dollar then and there, only I aint have to."

"Well, you aint paying for this one neither?"

"I aint mind."

"You know who is?"

"Who?"

"Willie, that who."

"Willie! Who twist off his arm?"

"No need. Mose Heywood he say he let Willie ride up in back of that old rust-out firetruck of his and smile and wave to the folks ifn he pay the bill, and Willie he take him up, only he having a couple sign hang down the sides the same. He say he need the advertising."

"He do, huh. Who he advertising for? He have the only store anyone go to."

"Well, all the same he want the signs, and that how come we a costume parade and a marching band, even it is just a high-school band from over the coast."

"Ever we need a mayor, he the only one go run."

"He running for it now."

And with that the voice-shadow it gone and Mama and Tramsee they laughing, and then come another shadow, and then some more laughing, and it been going on like that so long they aint never go see or either hear that marching band, only time they come to that bridge they be looking on someone else to blame. Ty he tire and thirst he waiting so long and he go inside, and then he back on the stoop with a warm Co-Cola in his hand from out the pantry and he saying say he aint mind none no sir he done heard plenty of marching bands in his time he aint go hurry about this one, only just then Mama and Tramsee they come stepping out the porch, and they both done heard what Ty just said. Before I knows what what Tramsee she all over Ty saying say what he mean about that crack aint he know this a regular brass horn marching band come all the way from over the coast and it aint go cost him a nickel to see it neither, and then what he doing a Co-Cola in his hand aint he enough sense to know he making people late sitting there drinking some and talk some like it a regular Saturday evening, and then Tramsee she shoving him off the stoop, and he trying to catch up a last swallow from out that bottle, only she shove him too hard and that bottle spill out in the grass. Mama she letting Tramsee do most of the talking and the shoving, but she angry just the same, and soon as Ty he up on his feet and walking down the walk, she shoving me the same.

Mama she wearing a blue shirtwaist, and you can see the cross of Jesus Christ hang round her neck, and Tramsee in something white seem to move around her whole body like air, and they both chewing they lips some about slow, monkey-butt men, and ifn they done miss that marching band, well, they aint know just what, but they is reliable for doing something, and that a fact. We lucky we aint been walking long before Mama she say hear that girl, and she talking to Tramsee, and it the marching band blowing brass, only we aint see it, and then Mama she looking back she saying say you catch up you want to but you stay out of trouble, you hear, and now she talking to me, and then Mama and Tramsee they hard feelings they melt off like hot butter and they running after that marching band, only it aint exactly running say it more like a twitching, and they aint looking back neither. Ty he watching them go, but mostly he watching Tramsee white behind twitching this way and that, and then mama and Tramsee they gone, and that white behind it gone the same, and me and Ty we left to walking by ourself.

"They sure is crazy," Ty say.

I aint know what to say so I aint say a word, and Ty he shake his head and laugh to hisself, and then he give me a narrow look and he start up again.

"You ever been with a woman, boy? I aint mean a little girl, now. I mean a full-growd woman. Tramsee she been a woman since she twelve year old. She what I mean."

"I been thinking on it."

"You is what? Boy you losing some valuable opportunity you spend all of you time thinking on it. I must of been with damn near forty women I old as you. Some of them girls too. I aint waste none of my time thinking on it." Then Ty he stop talking, like maybe he thinking on it all the same, and then he give me a eye full up with confoundment and exaggeration. "Boy, you making me thirsty something more than a Coke."

Time we up to the square, the festival lights they already on. The parade it done with, and most the folks they done circle back to the tables. I aint see Mama or either Tramsee for too many folks, but there Willie in front of the barbecue, and he smoke-shouting for everybody step on up and get some, and some they doing just that, and some they knocking about in the street and talking, and some they sucking down oysters or they eating a piece a pecan pie, and there all kind of laughter coming from the center of the square, only what it about I dont know, and Ty he walking past the tables and the laughter and the smell of barbecue smoke, and then he stopping in front of the volunteer firehouse, and I is stopping the same.

Five or six volunteer they sitting back on some rickety wooden chairs they done pull up to the edge of the street, and they got they feet prop up on some old wood crates and they drinking and talking and some they smoking and some they checking out the people go by. Aint much else to the place. The firetruck it back now from the parade been park up alongside the house maybe ten minute, but it still have them two sign hanging down the sides saying "Buy From Willie." It aint really a firetruck, just a old Ford pickup they done load up with a couple three ladder and some axes and a rust-out water tank almost empty in the back and about fifty foot of hose. The firehouse itself it just a one-story white cement block with a couple door been painted black and a couple three window cut out and that it, except there a small black bell hang on the wall out front for ringing ever there is a fire.

"How do you do, Ty?"

"How do you do, Mose," Ty say.

"Where you been?"

"Aint been anywhere different, tell you that."

"You want some of this here bottle," and Mose he pouring some rye straight down his throat.

"You done read my mind."

Then Ty he sitting on one of them rickety old chairs hisself and he drinking and smoking same as all the rest, aint no one talking now, and I sitting on the ground, my feet curl up beneath my knees, and Im is looking up to them volunteers and watching what goes. Aint nothing happen for a while. Then Mose he pull a deck of cards from out his back pocket and he slap it down direct on top of one of them crates.

"Who in," he say. Then the rest of them volunteers they all pulling they chairs up around that crate they saying say they in they go win them some hard cold cash before the night over, and Ty he saying he in the same, only he looking down he asking me how much change I brung, he know I a pocketful of dimes, but he aint say another word neither he just holding out his hand, and before I knows what what my pocket it empty, and Ty he playing poker with seven eight week of my working Mr. Fludds truck farm, and every now and then he throw a dime into the pot.

I is wondering how long I go be there before Ty give me my money back, but Ty he aint even look at me he so busy raking in pot after pot. Some of them volunteers they mumbling say maybe he good with cards but what about women, and then they giving Ty a sour mean look, but Ty he in such a good mood all he do is smile and rake in some more. Then Mose he start passing round another bottle of rye, and Ty he about to faint from waiting he want to feel that rye go down his throat, and then he doing just that, and that bottle going round and round and around, and Im is hoping Ty go shovel me some of my dimes before that bottle go round again, cause there a good chance he go forget about the game it do, but he aint pay me no mind at all.

Aint long before Ty he talking while he playing, he talking back to when he was in the United States Marines up at Montford Point, and them volunteers they just nodding they heads and letting him talk on and on. Ty he saying say the first day he come to boot camp, the sergeant, his name was Whitlow, he come on up to Ty and ask him did he like full grown women or little girls or maybe both, and Ty he was grinning with that, his teeth they was press down around his tongue, and he was saying say where was they at and how many and he like em both kinds every inch they head to they feet only he aint never make it all the way to they feet, and then Ty he was laughing with that, only Sergeant Whitlow he didnt see the joke, he start barking up in Ty face about how there wunt no women nearby, no little girls neither, how there wunt go be no one talk about the female half for the next eight week maybe more, wunt no one even think about them neither less he give out permission, and was about then Ty he start getting weak in the knees, and he was praying to the good Lord say dont let it be true Lord not eight week Lord knows he aint never been without a woman that long not since the day he was born, only the praying it didnt do no good.

The next seven week Ty and the rest of them boys they was marching all over the sandy flats and into the pine woods and up and down hills, and then they was wading through all kind of creeks and ponds, and then more woods or maybe a bog, and tripping over vines and pushing they way through briers and blood on they hands, and it was bad enough living in a tent city in them ten-man tents, never mind the flies biting you up and down, or maybe you walking in a black black creek and you falling into a trout hole you aint know how to swim somebody has to pull you out, and the next thing you know you sitting up under some birch pine and you shivering from cold and eating supper out a K-ration tin, and then the tin it empty and you back at it. Seem like all they was ever go do in the marines was march, even it raining, and when it wunt raining the sun it was laying on hot and thick like barbecue smoke, and the boys was all dragging, and then dragging some more, and they arms they was dropping to they sides, and then Sergeant Whitlow he was telling them all say they aint raise they arms keep them rifle butts over they monkey-butt heads they go be marching the whole night through, and then those arms they was coming up, look like everybody want to surrender, but they didnt know to who. It wunt at all like Ty done bargain for, the rest neither, but they all kept to it, only there wunt a day gone by Ty he wunt thinking about a woman, and he say the rest of them leather-heads they must of been thinking on women the same the way they was talking into they bedrolls every night. Wunt hardly no one getting no sleep at all.

Well by and by them boys they was fed up to here, it didnt matter there was only three day left of them sorry eight week, and there they was sitting on they cots or stretch out and they was all of them tired from marching sixteen hour. Some was saying how they wouldnt mind it none if them yellow Japs come all the way to North Carolina, if they wouldnt make em do all this marching, the Germans neither, they got there first. Some was saying there wunt no such thing as the Japs or the Germans, that was something made up to keep them out in the field, no, the only enemy they had to worry about was the United States Marines. Then a couple was saying say it was Sergeant Whitlow to blame, he didnt have no idea what he was doing, hell he was a private hisself ten week before, then a couple more they was saying hell it could a been worse, but the first two didnt think so, and then just like that the four of them was going at it on the ground. Then this big brown boy call Icebox Pete he break it up, and them four was back on they cots, and then Icebox he was saying say he just hope he get a hold of the sergeant just one time take his head clean off, and if he didnt swallow it up in one bite it sure as hell wouldnt take more than two.

Ty he wunt so full of outright pugnation like Icebox, but all the same he was tire of the marching and thinking he go on over the fence that very night maybe head on down to Charleston, just for the weekend, he knowd a couple of pretty girl there, only he aint seen them in a while. He aint never had the chance. Soon as he think that Sergeant Whitlow come into the tent, and this time it a surprise inspection and the sergeant he was looking at a couple footlocker, only they didnt measure up so he turn them over dump everything out he was saying say maybe they do a better job they start from scratch, and then he was walking up and down some more and smacking the palm of his hand with a swagger stick and all the while his tongue was running up around his mouth like he a mad dog licking foam, and then he was telling them boys say they wunt never go measure up, none of them they keep on disregarding regulations, no, he was go teach them once and for all, they had fifteen minute, then they better be outside with full-packs and rifles, they was going on a little march, maybe take part in some maneuvers, the whole damn camp was turning out.

Whitlow he march them boys down across some river and into the black of some river marsh, and they must of been out in that black black muck the better part of the night, and they hadnt seen or either heard of nothing but some gray hoot-owls talking death, and the sloshing of they feet, and maybe some moaning, and some they done figure they was marching straight into South Carolina, maybe they was heading for Charleston anyway, and some, the ones worry about them owls, they was for turning back right then, and some they just figure to find a good place to stop, have something to eat or just lie down, and then they come up from the water to a sandy, grassy flat stretch cover up with mostly pine, and them boys why they stop right there. Whitlow he come on back for a look see what what, look like he want to kick everybody head in too, only he knew he was too small, so he was telling them all he say you all better pick up you rifles and you packs and get a move on you hear aint no time to wait any of you monkey-butt boys thinking the other way I go bounce you out of this outfit so fast you think you back in the jungle. Whitlow he was shouting loud as he was able, only them boys they wunt none of them listening, they was lean theyself back against them pines and some they was falling asleep, and Whitlow he was about to pull a gun, only just then Icebox Pete he was standing up look down at the little man.

"Aint none of them boys gonna foot it no more till they had some rest. They dead like dogs." And then Icebox Pete he done ruffle up his shoulders so he was big as he could be, which was more than enough empty out Whitlow courage, and then he was saying, "You aint like it none, you going through me."

Whitlow he was looking up to Icebox Pete, only he wunt smiling with what Pete done said, but he wunt saying nothing neither cause he didnt relish the idea of going through that big brown boy, so he stood there underneath them pines and he was sputtering to hisself the while, and then Icebox he decide he done spend enough time in the woods he want a real bed under his back, even it only a cot in a tent, and with that he say come on, and then him and the boys they was heading back. Whitlow he wunt so much a fool as he a little man, but all the same he was following those boys through them pines, and all the while he was planning what to do about Icebox Pete and the rest, and telling them so too, how maybe they'd be breaking up rock the rest of they natural lives, but only if they was lucky, but every now and then he was telling them say he didnt mean what he said he forget the whole thing they just turn theyselves around and follow him some more, only wunt none of them listening, and Whitlow he was about to pull his gun again, maybe use it on hisself, only just then the sky was rip open with light and smoke, and a couple three shell come crashing down through the trees.

Icebox he was the first to hit the ground, and the rest of them boys they done the same, only then the air it was raining with hundreds of them shells, look like the sky was bleeding to death, and then there was some more shells and some more blood, and with that them boys they was running like hogs every which way look around for someplace to hide, wunt no one particular, and after a while wunt nothing to see but smoke. Ty he was the only one wunt cover up, and he was wiping the smoke from his eyes and wondering what he was go do, and then he done seen a oak tree been rip up from the roots and it look like a good enough place crawl to and hide, only was just then a shell burst over his head, and that was that, cause the next thing happen he was waking up in a hospital room.

Ty he thought he was in heaven, cause everywhere he look he seen white, and he wouldnt of been surprise to see

Peter hisself coming through the door and he was thinking what to say what all done happen how he wunt look as bad as all that, maybe Peter just hold him up to the light see his good side, but the next thing he seen wunt no angel at all, was a crop-hair nurse standing up by his bed with a basin in one hand and two towel in the other. She was waiting on Ty to open his mouth, only Ty he couldnt get a word out he looking at that nurse, and she seen he was having trouble so she was telling him say he must of had one sweet angel watch over him cause by rights he should of been dead, and Ty he was asking the nurse what she was talking about, only she didnt answer except to say how she wunt the doctor she wunt go talk about what happen it a too too delicate matter he just have to wait, and with that she done set the basin on the bed table and then she took up a towel and full it up with soapy water, and then she was washing Ty all over.

Ty he was a bit confuse and tire, but he sure didnt mind what that crop-hair nurse was doing, and by and by he was feeling pretty good. He didnt remember the last time a woman been touch him like that, it didnt matter how old she was, but all the same it seem to Ty there was something missing, and with that he was sitting up on his elbows and smiling at the nurse try and catch her eye, but she wunt interested, and even she was laughing some to herself, and then Ty seen why. He could see where she was washing, and there wunt nothing there except her hands and the towel and the soap and his own two skinny leg. There wunt even a char-black stub grab hold of for luck, and when Ty seen that, well he wunt sitting up no more. He let his head fall straight back to the pillow, and then a black-ice look come full up his eyes.

The nurses at that hospital they was as nice as they could be, and bringing him soups and sometimes a piece of peach pie, and every morning they'd be washing him down but good, and sometimes they'd just come for relax and some talk, but by and by, Ty he was done with the hospital and them free-talking nurses, and then he was standing up along side the rest of his squad in a oak-panel room. They was all line up, and Ty he figure they was all about to get theyself a court martial, running out like they did with Icebox Pete, and he was waiting on Sergeant Whitlow come in and then they go hear the worst for sure, only it was this square-jaw captain instead, and he was talking how sad he was they walk into them shells, there wunt suppose to be no artillery for two or three more hour, someone got the times mixed up, but they done showed they was first rate the way they handled theyself been wounded like that, he was proud of them all, like they was his own, and Ty he was looking around some more for Whitlow and hoping he didnt show up just yet, cause he knowd the sergeant have something more to say, but then the captain he was talking how sad he was about Sergeant Whitlow, it was a damn dirty shame he been kill dead by them shells, and the only one too, he'd have been proud like the captain, wunt too many sergeants have a whole squad getting they purple hearts, didnt matter it wunt exactly the enemy, the captain he'd seen to that, and then he was talking how he was go find out who give the order on that artillery, even it the last thing he ever do, cause men like the good Sergeant Whitlow they was hard to come by. Then the captain was done with his talk and pinning on medals, and then he give them boys a white-glove salute, and then they was all out the door.

Ty he done talking now, and the volunteers they all nodding they heads like they done got purple hearts pin to they shirts the same, and then Mose he say for everyone to ante up a dime, and with that Ty he looking down at his pile of change, only there aint no pile, cause all the while Ty been talking he been losing, and then he looking down at me again and he asking me say you any more change, and I say I dont, and then Mose he say again for everyone to ante up a dime. Ty he give Mose a hard look with that, and look like Mose he turning blue too, only he dont say another word, and then Ty he the one look discomfort and disbelief in that blueface silence, dont know what he go do, and then he reach into his pocket and pull out his purple heart and he lay it on the crate. Well right off some of them volunteers they asking Ty what he do that for, that his only medal, whyunt he take it up, forget about this here poker game and sleep it off, he only lost a pocketful of dimes and they wunt even his to begin with, but Ty he full of determination now so much so he almost shake, and then that blueface Mose he asking what it worth he always wanted one hisself but he never got the chance they bounced him out of boot camp the very first week, and Ty he nod his head and then he saying say it worth more than the crown jewels of the state of South Carolina. Aint no one know what he mean by that so aint no one say a word, and then that blueface Mose he nod his head and deal up the cards, there aint no more betting this time on account of Ty, and then everybody spreading they cards out face up on the crate have a look see whats what, only Ty he more hesitate and expectation than the rest, and just like that Mose he break into a blueface smile and then he raking in the pot, and the last thing he do he fix that medal to his shirt. Poor old Ty. He just staring at the cards, he aint move or either say a word, and when Mose see that he reach over give Ty a bottle all to hisself, even it almost half full, and with that Ty he up from that rickety old chair, and he look around a moment like he see or either hear someone he know come across the square, only aint no one there, and then he sidle up to where that old Ford firetruck it hunker down and he climbing in with all them ladders and axes and that fifty foot hose, and then he tip his head back and start pouring that sweet rye liquor down his sorry sorry throat.

The next thing that happen Im is walking from the firehouse to the square wish on something to eat, and I know I aint never go see my dimes again so I just put it out of my mind, and I just up to the barbecue grill when this voice it come and full up my ears with a rustle feel like smoke. It Jonas Lee, and he standing up under a string of white light he swaying back and forth and back and forth, cause he up on some crutches, and he laughing all the while like he go beat the tar out the devil his hide on account of he has hisself another idea.

I know the best thing to do is keep on walking cause Jonas he trouble and Mama she tell me say keep away from trouble before she done run off after that marching band, but Mama she aint here, and Jonas he is, and before I thinking what what we both walking down along the square to Front Street, and then we standing up front of Willies. I knows what Jonas he wanting now, cause we been here before, he wanting to get inside. Willies it a whitewash dry-goods turn liquor store out front, and a two-story weather-beat warehouse been add on out back, only aint nothing up on the second floor but some old newspaper, some empty cans, and some empty bottle Willie been collect the last ten year. Me and Jonas we been try to get inside a couple three time, but Willie he always come up behind. Jonas he saying this here maybe our best chance cause Willie he eating barbecue, and before he say another word we both around back in the alley have a look. There a small flatbed wagon shove up against a double black door and a couple black-out window up the second floor, and Jonas he saying say all we do we pull that wagon up under there, and he pointing to one of them window, and then we climb up and in, and Jonas he so impress with hisself he almost fall over his crutches. I has to say he a pretty good plan, but Im is wishing it was more better cause I knows Jonas he aint go be pulling or climbing cause he on them crutches, and besides, he too small to reach up to them windows even he standing on two three wagon piggyback.

Aint nothing come easy. I has my hands wrap around the hitch of that wagon, and I pulling and pulling, only the wagon it aint move to breathe, and Jonas he saying say what the matter what I doing now why dont I quit my fooling and do like he say, and I like to knock Jonas his mouth shut right there, only I too busy pulling, and what keeping it I aint know cause the wagon it empty but feel like a team of mule dug in at the other end, maybe worse, maybe it the devil hisself dug in, and Im is thinking say maybe I better give up while I can cause aint nobody win against the devil, and that what I about to do, only just then the wagon it pull loose with a lurch, and I is landing in the alleydirt. Jonas he laughing now and over to the wagon he bend on down, and then he holding up a piece of chain link iron and he saying say this here what you been pull against it chain up to the side only it broke now, and then he laughing some more, and I feels like maybe I should knock him around double, only I dont. Then I pulling that wagon to one of them black-out windows and Jonas he pointing the one he want, and then Im is climbing up. Willie he done put in a brand new pane of glass, but he left it up, so I grab a hold of the sill and then I poking my head inside, and Jonas all he can do he saying say what you see anybody there what it is, but aint nothing to see cause it too dark. Then Jonas he saying he gone go around front and wait on me to open the door, and with that he hobble off, and I hears the scratch scratch scratch of his crutch on the gravel as he go, and then I aint hear it no more, and then I climbs on in.

It too dark to see much of anything, so I hugging close to the wall with every step. Im is walking through some newspaper scatter on the floor, and I kick a couple three empty can smell like coffee grounds, and then Im is coming to a gray box shadow, which turn out it the stairs, and the next thing I sees is Jonas Lee and he at the front door and grinning like some poor Joe strutting around the marsh found hisself something to eat, and he saying say come on come on, so I lets him in, and then we looking up at the shelves see what what. It aint hard to see now cause the light from the festival it pouring through the plate glass windows out front like soft yellow smoke. There everything from glycerol cream to red bricks to beans to hand soap and potatoes, but we aint after none of that, and then Jonas Lee he stop he pointing to some shelves in the back, and there twenty maybe twenty-five carton of fireworks line up in a row.

Jonas he saying say them fireworks they time has come, and with that then Im is grabbing hold of them cartons and stack em up by the door, and Jonas he saying hurry on up hurry on up aint no telling about Willie he might be footing it over maybe get hisself something to drink, and I trying not to listen to Jonas Lee cause sometime he a aggravating way about him, but all the same Im is thinking how what we doing go cost something, and what I go do if Willie come through that door, and I almost drop a couple carton with that only I dont, and then them cartons they all stack up by the door. The next thing Jonas Lee saying say where that flatbed we better move along while we can, only by we he mean just me on account of his leg, so I around to the back go pull that wagon to the front, and then I loading up. It one thing break into the back of a store come night maybe see Willie ghost hover up in the dark, it another load up with twenty twenty-five carton been stole up under the festival eye, and look like Jonas he thinking the same thing cause he keeping a lookout for Willie or either anyone else come along from the square. Every now and then he waving his crutch in the air, which mean stop, so I does, and when he satisfy aint nobody seen us he wave for me to start up again, which I does that too, and then the cartons they all up on the wagon, and Jonas Lee he hop up into the front and then he sitting, his broken leg prop up against the hitch, and his crutches laying up by his side.

Jonas Lee he say the best place to shoot off them fireworks is on the other side of the square by them live oaks lean out over the Governors Wall, so thats where we heading. Then he say what he would and wouldnt give see Willie face time we fire his rockets, and then he laughing some, and then he saying say it a swampblack sky we about to full up with some jolly-roger smoke outdo even Willie his barbecue, and then he laughing some more, and the more and more Jonas he talk to hisself, the more better he impress hisself the same. We a long way to go, but by and by we come to the other side of the wall, and that wagon it pull up under a big old live oak with moss hang down. I is already tired. It have the feeling like my arms still rolling with that wagon, and I is thinking maybe I should stretch out and sleep, but Jonas Lee he have other ideas. He hobbling through the grass now and he saying say what you doing now aint go be no show we dont set it up, and with that I is lining up them rockets, and it don't take too long, but long enough, and then Jonas he say it sure go be something, and then he shove a couple box of matches into my hands and slip behind one of them oaks and aint nothing but his two eyes blinking out through the moss.

Well I is looking at Jonas a moment, and it come to me again what we doing go cost something, but I shake it off. Then Im is looking to the flatbed wagon and the shadow of the wall and them fireworks line up and that box of matches, and I aint know if I angry or either scare, but something inside of me about to bust out, and with that then Im is striking them matches, maybe one for every five or six rocket, and them rocket tail tips they glowing red and hissing and spitting, sound like snakes, only I aint bother none cause I moving down the line, and then I done with them matches and I double up behind the wall go watch a couple three hundred snake hissing and twisting they way through a swampblack sky.

I aint never seen nothing like it. Like God hisself laughing at the world. Some of the rockets they aint go up high enough and they clipping folks up one side and down the other, and some they angle too high and they is heading for the low side of the square down along the Front Street stores, and there all kinds of dogs yapping they heads, and some of the folks they yapping they heads the same, and some look like they bleeding with the light from them rockets and then down on they knees and they praying the

Lord go take them up cause seem like maybe it judgement day at last, and the ones from that marching band they aint marching now they all running to the dock, and aint but a couple three hang on to they instruments cause there all kind of horns and drums and pipes and even a brass tuba been left in the grass, they gone, but most of the peoples they running back and forth across the square, and back and forth again, and tripping over horns and such and cursing, they all in a panic like pigs, aint nobody have no idea what they doing or either where they is, and then Im is thinking say there aint no reason be standing by a couple empty box say fireworks on the side, and Jonas Lee he must of come to the same conclude cause he already gone.

The smoke it just starting to lift, and I see a shadow-crowd of people gather down along Front Street, and then I hear a couple shadow-voice come floating through the air, and they talking hush and disbelief.

"It a damn shame it go up like this."

"He wunt but eating his barbecue twenty minute ago, now look what happening."

"Who you think done it?"

"Dont know."

Then Im is pushing my way up to the front of the crowd see what what, and everybody looking at Willies, which it on fire now, and they all watching the fire grow higher, higher, and then a couple more voice they mumbling by my ear.

"It aint them fireworks thats the cause of all this infernal combustion."

"It sure aint."

"We oughta be out there right now looking see who set em off. He cant be too far."

"He aint have no sense, tell you that much. Didnt he know the wind catch that fire, spread it around some of them stores, they all be melting like butter."

"Someone oughta be looking."

"Oughta be is right. But what you go do?"

"Aint that the truth."

I aint hardly move the while they talking, I aint want to give myself away, and then they done and we all watching Willie his warehouse burn. Seem like the fire done eat out the black of that swampblack sky with a couple three hundred red and yellow tongue licking up and out, but aint nobody move cause they watching the same as me till the bell from the firehouse it clang clang clang clang, and with that then the peoples they move a couple step back and that old Ford pickup come rolling by, and then it stop, and it still has them two sign hanging down say "Buy From Willies."

Mose Heywood he the first volunteer off the truck, he still wearing that medal, and he telling folks say stand back stand back, and then the rest of them volunteers they jumping off the same, and some they out with they ladders and they axes, though what good ladders and axes go do aint no one know cause that fire it burning so hot aint nothing to see pretty soon but ash, and Mose he trying to hook up the hose to the water pump, only every time he pull on that hose it pulling him back the same. What it is there a body curl up in the back of that Ford, and that body it Ty, and he tangle up in that fifty foot hose, he hugging a empty bottle too, and look like he aint about to wake up even he been on fire hisself. Every time Mose he give a pull, he rolling Ty forward, and then Ty his dead weight pull his ownself back, so Mose he aint getting nowhere. All the same it take him five or six pull make him convince, and then he looking in back and see Ty tangle up, and then he call the rest of them volunteers and then they all tugging and tugging at poor old Ty, seem like nothing go make him budge, and then all of a sudden, Ty he come flying through the air, it lucky a couple of them volunteer they catch him, and that fifty foot hose come rolling off the truck.

Them volunteers they done lay Ty down in the dust of the square with that and then they working get a hold of that hose, and some from that shadow-crowd they looking at Ty and shaking they heads with disengagement and they saying say what he doing the back of that truck he cover up with so much liquor he reliable catch on fire hisself well that what come of folk like him yes sir he and that Tramsee girl they should of been a law against folk like that coming here dirty up our town, and look like a couple three they about to kick Ty in the head, only is just then Willie his whole place seem to heave up a shudder like it go explode, and then it does, and then everybody down on they knees they cover up they heads cause here come a flock of bust up wood and bottle glass and window glass and some broken plates, and even some wicker baskets, and all of that come sweeping over the street and then down, and then maybe five six hundred potato sweep down the same, only it aint sweep exactly cause them potatoes aint small, and they coming pretty hard, and knock some people out too, and then someone saying say the fire must of got to all that liquor aint nothing feed a fire like whiskey and rye, and some they looking to the fire with that, like they wouldnt mind being fed some whiskey and rye they ownself, but aint nobody move from they knees, not even them volunteers.

The next thing happen Mose Heywood he standing in front of that old Ford pickup and he calling for help, and then some of them volunteers they climbing up on top pump out some water, and some they holding on to that fifty foot hose, and Mose he pointing the way, only nothing come out but a snake-squirt of water, which the fire it just swallow up, and they give a couple three more squirt, only each time they do the fire open it mouth and swallow some more. Everybody they back to they feet now, aint nothing to do but watch Willie warehouse burn to the ground, and some they saying it a awful thing, they glad they aint him, but it sure do look pretty, dont it, and some they saying say it a shame some of them other buildings dont catch, aint nothing in em, and they nothing but eyesores anyhow, and then all of a sudden aint no one talking, except maybe to theyself, and they taking a couple step back, some one way, some the other, and from out the shadow of they faces come Willie hisself, and he stop in back of them volunteers, they still feeding they snake-water to that fire, and he breathing heavy, and look like his eyes go fall out of his head.

Willie he furious and uncontrol at first, he looking up at the fire and the smoke, and pressing his hands up to his rumple-up bald head like he trying to squeeze a orange, but by and by he feel the folks they eyes prick up against his back, and he know he have a crowd waiting on him to talk the talk, and with that then he climbing into the back of that old Ford pickup he face up the crowd. Then he open his mouth and the words they come rolling out, they black like the smoke billow up from his warehouse, and Willie he saying say the devil he the one done all of this here the work of the devil it always been mark by fire ever since the Jews they done left the Pharaoh look at this here fire look it you aint never seen a fire so bright as that so red it red like blood you aint never seen the sky bleed like this no you aint but it bleeding now and that the sign of the devil sure as you and me standing here only what we go do about it the devil he go swallow up this whole island with fire we let him so what we go do we aint do nothing.

Everybody know what come next cause Willie he aint never talk about the devil he dont get around to old man Thaddeus, and when he do it hard not to believe he talking truth the way he get everybody work up. He talking anger and revenge now, and everybody listening they all full up with angry and revengement, even they aint know they feel it. Then Willie he open his mouth again nail them folks eyes and ears back to the bone, and with every word come rolling out of his mouth he bigger, bigger, bigger, and pretty soon he big as the fire itself, and with that I aint sure maybe I dead or either dream cause   *Willie his bald rumple head*

*it curl up under the black-burn thatch of the sky, and his
words they sounding like the voice of God sit in judgement,
and Willie his eyes they burning brighter, brighter with the
snake-dance flick of that fire, and everywhere he look folks
they all falling dead to the ground, they all burn up aint
nothing left but a pile of ash and some bone, and Willie he
saying say we done burn the devil burn him right out of
them folks, and I aint move to breathe cause I waiting he
turn his snake-dance eyes on me and thinking say what it
feel like be burn to ash and bone, only Willie he aint look
my way cause he happy enough for burning the rest of them
gather-up folk, and some they done try to run, they fighting
the urge of them fire-happy words, but they burn up all the
same, and then they all burn except me, and Willie he open
up a cat-shriek mouth and laugh with that, and he laughing
say he done burn the devil from out of his tree aint no
where the old man devil he climb to now, only then Willie
he aint laughing no more, look like he cover up with fire,
and then all I see is a shadow use to been Willie and a
piece of that fire it break off and I sees it the devil, and then
the devil and Willie they both have at it, they wrestling
harder, harder, harder, and Willie he cat-shriek some more
he the devil in his hands now and he aint about to let go,
and then the devil he throwing Willie to the black wood-ash
what left of the warehouse floor, and then old Willie he
back on his feet and it his turn throw the devil, and the fire
burning brighter and brighter, and Willie and the devil they
rolling this way and that through the flames and back to
they feet only aint no one turn the advantage yet, and then*

it look like the devil he a grip around Willie neck but then Willie he has the same grip, and then Willie and the devil they gone, like they been swallow up, and all what left is a devil-eating fire burn my eyes, and maybe I know better, and maybe I dont, but all the same Im is stretching myself up to that fire to look at it, to know it, talk it, breathe it, taste it, only just then a voice it grab me from behind, and then the fire it gone the same.

"Say, boy. You sure as hell aint gonna find what you looking for in there."

And with that it like I been wake from the dead, and I looking up, and there the pasty white face of old man Thaddeus hisself, only aint no expression to his eyes, and he done caught me up around my collar with two hand and he dragging me back from the smoking black wood and the glass and the brick, and then we back to the grass edge of the square like we waiting on something to happen. "This a better place," he say. "You see what you want from here, and then we moving on."

Most the peoples they done give up watching now and they walking back across the square in twos and threes look like clouds of smoke drifting up through the haze of them festival lights, and then they gone, but some they still shaking they heads they saying they glad they aint Willie it a god damn shame a fire swallow up everything a man own what God he have in mind let something like that happen must of had something in mind but wunt it a good show all the same it sure was that, and then they looking around maybe grab some half-cook potatoes before they head off, and then there the volunteers they all cover up with black wood-ash hard to see who who, but they too sleep-hungry mind about that and packing up that Ford with they ladders and they axes and they fifty foot tangle hose, and the last thing they lifting into the back is Ty hisself, look like nothing go wake him up a fire dont, and they cover him up with one of those signs say "Buy From Willies," and then they all rolling on back to the firehouse.

The only thing left still burning is Willie, only he walking hush and intent through the hot hot ash and the black wood chips and the soft smell of burn whiskey linger on, and all the while he mumbling to hisself about he aint done yet take more than a little fire to finish him off thats what it was a little fire no he the one go finish off that old man and it dont matter he the devil not one little bit, and then Willie he see me and the old man standing back in the grass, aint nobody move or either say a word we watching each other a while, and then Willie he squatting down into the thick of the wood and whiskey ash, he watching the smoke float straight up into the sky, and over and over and over he saying the devil, the devil, the devil.